"Please tell me why you are acting like this."

"Don't push me, Hayley," Jackson said through gritted teeth.

Don't push him? "You are in my house, bossing me about and rearranging my stuff. And I'm the one who's being pushy?"

"No, you're the reason why I'm taking cold showers lately. And they haven't helped a damn!"

What was he talking ab—oh. Oh.

Jackson pushed both hands into his hair and tugged. "You're driving me nuts."

His words, uttered in that deep, sexy growl, dialed her heat factor back up to a thousand degrees. She had to be in his arms, she needed to have his lips on hers, she couldn't wait any longer to know how he tasted, whether reality came close to her imagination.

Jackson took a step back and raised his hand in a "stay there" gesture. "I'm going to go."

What? Noooooooo! Why? Things were just getting interesting.

"I thought you were going to kiss me," Hayley whispered.

Jackson scrubbed his hands over his face. "God, I want to."

"So what's the problem?"

* * *

How to Handle a Heartbreaker by Joss Wood is part of the Texas Cattleman's Club: Fathers and Sons series.

Dear Reader,

Welcome to the second book in the Texas Cattleman's Club: Fathers and Sons series!

Independent and fiery, Hayley Lopez has a busy life. As the youngest child and only daughter of an overprotective oil baron, she has struck out on her own and works as a sheriff's deputy for the Royal sheriff's department. She's studying toward her law degree and offers legal advice to the less fortunate residents of Royal. She does not need a man in her life, especially one who is trying to develop the area around Stone Lake, an area of Royal she adores.

Jackson Michaels is a billionaire real estate developer, and thirteen years older than Hayley. He's impressed that he doesn't intimidate her but uncomfortable with his attraction to the much younger woman and their off-the-charts chemistry.

They agree to a no-strings fling, but things soon become complicated when they both catch feelings.

I hope you enjoy reading *How to Handle a Heartbreaker* as much as I enjoyed writing it. It truly was a superfun book to write. Connect with me on Facebook at josswoodbooks, on Twitter at josswoodbooks and on BookBub at joss-wood.

Happy reading!

Joss

JOSS WOOD

HOW TO HANDLE A
HEARTBREAKER

HARLEQUIN
DESIRE

Special thanks and acknowledgment are given to Joss Wood for her contribution to the Texas Cattleman's Club: Fathers and Sons miniseries.

HARLEQUIN®

DESIRE™

ISBN-13: 978-1-335-73529-4

How to Handle a Heartbreaker

Recycling programs for this product may not exist in your area.

Harlequin Enterprises ULC
22 Adelaide St. West, 40th Floor
Toronto, Ontario M5H 4E3, Canada
www.Harlequin.com

Printed in U.S.A.

Joss Wood loves books, coffee and traveling—especially to the wild places of southern Africa and, well, anywhere. She's a wife and a mom to two young adults. She's also a slave to two cats and a dog the size of a small cow. After a career in local economic development and business, Joss writes full-time from her home in KwaZulu-Natal, South Africa.

Books by Joss Wood

Harlequin Desire

Murphy International

One Little Indiscretion
Temptation at His Door
Back in His Ex's Bed

Texas Cattleman's Club: Fathers and Sons

How to Handle a Heartbreaker

Harlequin Presents

South Africa's Scandalous Billionaires

How to Undo the Proud Billionaire
How to Win the Wild Billionaire

Visit her Author Profile page at Harlequin.com, or josswoodbooks.com, for more titles.

You can also find Joss Wood on Facebook, along with other Harlequin Desire authors, at Facebook.com/harlequindesireauthors!

One

He's here.

Hayley Lopez scowled at the text message on her phone from Bubba Conor and knew the "he" was the bullying billionaire Jackson Michaels. Michaels, Royal's most successful real estate developer, had been harassing her client for the past month, demanding he sell his well-situated parcel of land on the edge of Stone Lake so that he could build a mixed-use estate on the edges of Stone Lake.

Well, technically, Bubba wasn't her client. He was just a lonely old widower she periodically checked on in her official capacity as one of Royal's sheriff's deputies. She had another year of law school until she could officially have clients but, until then, she was faking it to make it and dispensing the little legal advice she could.

She had a ton of work and didn't have time to visit Bubba's property to have a chat with Jackson Michaels. But Bubba, mild-mannered and shy, needed a representative, and Hayley could tell Michaels, forcefully, that Bubba had no desire to sell his smallholding.

Maybe then Jackson Michaels would get the message.

She'd also tell him that Royal didn't need a mixed-use development spoiling the serene and tranquil lake. Families camped at the lake, fished there. Lovers— young, old and sometimes illicit—made out there. At a recent community meeting, the residents of Royal made it clear that they weren't keen on any developments at Stone Lake. The developer, damn his stubborn soul, had yet to back down.

Hayley loved Stone Lake. Her grandparents were once Bubba's closest neighbors. She'd spent most summers in her swimsuit on the water, fishing and swimming and canoeing. She loved the peace of the area and hated the idea of a multistory hotel and cottages, all generic and boring, on the edge of the lake.

Ugh. Hayley pulled on her seat belt, jammed her sunglasses over her eyes—designer and a gift from her older brother for her birthday—and headed out of town. She appreciated the gift because there was no way she could afford a pair on her cop salary; between feeding herself and paying for law school, making ends meet was enough of a challenge as it was.

You can always run home to Daddy...

Hayley scoffed at her inner voice, knowing she had more chance of falling pregnant by celestial intervention—as she wasn't currently enjoying a red-hot affair—than of her running home to Mom and Dad.

Juan Lopez, a billionaire oil baron and complete control freak, would love that and she had no intention of falling into line like her three older brothers. No, like her father, she preferred doing things her way. The hard way, her mom told her, but if hard meant her freedom, then she'd take it over being dictated to.

"You are too ambitious..."

"You are too up-front..."

"You are too independent..."

Remembering the words frequently lobbed at her by her parents, and her older brothers, Hayley scowled.

"You are never going to find a man, settle down."

Hayley released a snort. Now there was a sentence her brothers never heard. No, her two single brothers— her eldest sibling was married with kids—were encouraged to play the field, to sow their wild oats. From cars to curfews to chores, there was one set of rules for her brothers, another set for her. They'd been allowed to study what they wanted at college, encouraged to chase their business dreams and to be as ruthlessly ambitious as they could be. In her brothers, ambition and drive were positive attributes but her parents expected her to settle down and marry to make babies instead of making a difference. Be protected instead of being the protector. Hayley tapped the butt of her Glock. Screw that. She wouldn't stand on the sidelines of life, waiting for some man to put a ring on her finger and to, supposedly, make her happy.

She was happy already. Okay, reasonably content. *Busy* was a better description. Crazy busy.

But at least she was master of her destiny.

Hayley swung into Bubba's driveway, taking it easy through the potholes and over the bumps in the road. As she approached the house, her heart stopped when she noticed the astonishingly expensive, limited-edition Ford 150 pickup lording over Bubba's battered Jeep. The matte black pickup was the latest of her dream cars, the one material object she lusted over...

If there was one thing that could tempt her to return to the family fold, it would be the ability to buy luxury vehicles. In fact, her father had tried to bribe her to return home with the offer of a new car, anything she wanted, no expense spared.

If she'd acquiesced, then a truck like this would be hers. But, when weighing her freedom versus a new set of wheels, freedom always won, hands down.

Hayley parked, exited her patrol car and pushed her sunglasses up onto the top of her head. Unable to resist, she ran her hand down the sleek line of the truck's hood and stood up on her tiptoes to look inside the interior.

"It has heated seats, an eight-inch touch screen, a Wi-Fi hot spot, and wireless device charging." A deep voice rolled over her and raised goose bumps on her skin. But while she appreciated the deep and dark tenor, the fact that he'd assume that she could only appreciate the pretties on his truck annoyed her.

"I'm more interested in the 450-horsepower twin-turbo V6 engine and its ten-speed automatic transmission," Hayley replied, her back still to him.

"A girl who likes cars. I'm impressed."

A girl? She might be young—she'd be turning twenty-four in a few months—but she wasn't a *girl*, for God's sake! Holy crap, could he sound more patronizing if he tried?

Hayley spun around, intending to nail him with an "it's Officer Lopez to you, dirtbag" look but, on catching a glimpse of all his golden wonderfulness, her tongue disconnected with her brain. Jackson Michaels stood in front of her, looking sinfully sexy in a black crew neck sweater and gray chinos, trendy trainers on his feet. Thick hair, the color of sunlight dancing on a cornfield, was expertly cut and styled. Someone with no imagination would call his eyes *blue* but it was such an insipid word for the various shades she saw in his eyes. *Sea blue* would be closer but on looking closer, she saw the hint of purple and decided they were the color of ripe blueberries, picked off the bush. Maybe they were the color of Texas bluebonnets… Whatever their shade, thick eyebrows and dark lashes complemented the blue.

Hayley, still trying to fill her lungs, took in his slightly hooked nose, his sexy mouth and the thick stubble over his strong jaw.

Jackson Michaels was, undeniably, hot.

Hayley, very reluctantly, pulled her eyes off his tall, muscled, athletic-as-hell body and looked past him to see Bubba scowling at her from his rickety porch. Right, she was here on business…

Best to remember that.

"Mr. Michaels, I am Officer Lopez," Hayley told him, trying to put a decent amount of frost into her voice. She had to remember that this man was trying to force Bubba off his land, to convert a pristine area into a pimped-up office block and residential estate with a golf course. *Ugh*.

"Yeah, Bubba said I was trespassing and that he called you."

He didn't look even a little intimidated. Damn him.

"Are you going to lay charges against me, Bubba?" Jackson asked, his eyes not leaving Hayley's face. Hayley resisted the urge to check whether her waist-length hair was still in its severe bun, whether any strands had come loose. She felt like she was under a microscope and she didn't like the sensation, not one bit...

But she could easily imagine him looking at her like that when she was naked... Now, that would be hot.

For God's sake, Lopez, get a grip.

"No, I'm not going to lay charges. Hayley, please tell him that I don't want to sell," Bubba demanded, the tip of his walking stick hitting the wooden planks on his porch.

"Mr. Conor doesn't want to sell, Mr. Michaels," Hayley said, keeping her voice bland. "Please stop harassing him."

Those eyes cooled a little... "I think *harassing* is too strong a word, Officer."

"You've made the offer, he's declined—" Hayley made a shooing gesture with her hands "—so you can leave."

Jackson grinned and Hayley knew he wasn't leaving anytime soon. "Is the crime rate so low in Royal that they are now sending officers to mediate civil disputes?"

Ah, this was always a tricky question to answer. Technically, she shouldn't be here and if Sheriff Battle heard that she'd made a stop at Bubba's, he'd rip her a new one. She had work to do and Bubba, fit and healthy, wasn't high on the list of his priorities.

Hayley wrinkled her nose, trying to find an explanation that would fly. Before she could speak, Bubba jumped into the conversation.

"Hayley is my lawyer."

Hayley winced. That wasn't, technically, true. It wasn't true at all. She was a sheriff's deputy studying for her law degree and she had no right to issue advice. But the undeserved, unseen and neglected citizens of Royal needed a champion and she couldn't stand by when they needed help. In fact, they were why she'd decided to study law. She wanted to become a Legal Aid lawyer, someone they could turn to when life became legally overwhelming.

Yeah, she'd inherited her father's protective nature but, unlike him, her "clients" had to ask for her help. She never assumed they were incapable.

"A lawyer and a cop," Jackson drawled, looking amused. "Quite the combination. How do you find time to do it all? Do you keep your Superwoman cape in the trunk of your car?"

Now he was just mocking her. Or was he? The light in his eyes suggested he was teasing but Hayley couldn't be sure. Besides, she was the law. She should be above being teased. She had a goddamn Glock on her hip and a shield on her belt.

But, because she *was* the law, she couldn't misrepresent herself. "I haven't taken the bar yet, and I make suggestions, I don't give advice. And if I did hand out advice, it would be unofficial."

Remembering her father's advice to her brothers—always portray confidence and show no fear—she refused to drop her eyes from his, not for a second. And, let's be honest here, why would she want to look away? He was gorgeous and a balm for her very tired eyes.

A lazy smile crossed his face. "What did the lawyer name his daughter?" He waited for a beat before hitting her with the punch line. "Sue."

A lawyer joke that was so corny she almost cracked a smile. She tipped her head to the side. "Have you seen the size of my weapon, Mr. Michaels?"

"It was an awful joke but not so bad to warrant a threat of violence." Yep, definitely amused.

"I didn't threaten violence. I asked you if you noticed my weapon. It's big, and spurts out big bullets that make big holes," Hayley tartly responded, watching Bubba slip back into his house.

His laugh danced on the cool November air. He peered at her name tag. "What does the *H* stand for? Helga? Hesta? Honoria?"

Honoria? Really? Hayley was still very tempted to pull out her gun and shoot him. But the paperwork would be a bitch and jail inconvenient. Decisions, decisions...

"I don't have time to spar with you, Mr. Michaels,"

Hayley said through gritted teeth. "Bubba doesn't want to sell, and you can't make him. From what I understand, his land is essential to your project so why don't you give up this idea of developing the area around Stone Lake and find somewhere else to spoil?"

Jackson remained slouched against his car. "I'm beginning to think you don't like me, Officer Harriet Lopez."

She did like him…no, wrong. She liked looking at him. His smart mouth? Not so much. Well, she wouldn't mind kissing that mouth…

Oh, God.

Hayley, just leave…

Hayley pushed her shoulders back and lifted her chin. "I'm asking you, nicely, to leave Bubba alone. He doesn't want to sell. Deal with it. Do not make me come out here again."

"Oh, I might. If I'm bored and I want some entertainment, Officer Hanna—"

Entertainment? She was his *entertainment*?

"Are you normally this patronizing and annoying, Mr. Michaels?"

Hayley felt her temper inch up at his blatant disregard for her and the work she did. How dared he assume that she had time to waste. That the most important part of her day was meeting him.

Jerk.

"I have more important things to do than trade inanities with you!" Her words felt hot leaving her mouth and she knew that, with just the slightest provocation, she might lose her shit.

Sheriff Battle would not be amused. He and her temper were old friends and he'd cautioned her, on more than one occasion, that it would one day get her into trouble.

Chill, Hayley.

"Do you know how busy I am, Mr. Michaels?" Hayley asked through gritted teeth.

"How busy are you, Helen?"

Hayley narrowed her eyes at Michaels, desperate to wipe that smug smile off his face. "Did you hear about the baby that was abandoned on the trunk of Cammie Wentworth's car in the Royal Memorial Hospital parking lot?"

Jackson nodded. "Of course I did. Cammie is a good friend of mine."

How good a friend? Were they sleeping together? Were they involved? She could see it. Cammie Wentworth was the daughter of Tobias Wentworth, a Texas Cattleman's Club stalwart and billionaire oil and cattle rancher. Jackson's father had been, apparently, Wentworth's best friend and after his son, Rafael, left Royal after falling out with his father, Michaels became Wentworth's de facto son.

Cammie and Jackson made perfect sense. But she'd seen Cammie with Drake... Honestly, keeping up with Royal gossip was exhausting.

Annoyed and jealous, and irritated at feeling annoyed and jealous, Hayley slapped her hands on her hips. "I have been working twelve-to-fourteen-hour days trying to find out who baby Pumpkin belongs to and you know how far I've got?"

"How far?"

"Nowhere! I've checked local birth records, have perused reports of missing infants and checked on whether any accident victims had a baby. I'm running out of ideas."

Jackson looked like he was about to speak so Hayley nailed him with an if-you-talk-you-die look. "I haven't had a decent night's sleep in a month and if my parents insist on introducing me to another man they think I should marry, I will throw up."

"Uh—"

"I have to study, I have assignments coming out of my ears and I'm falling behind. I'm not the falling-behind type."

"I'm sure—"

She wasn't done. Not until he understood why she didn't have time to waste. "I can't even use my crazy life and insane schedule to get out of going to the TCC gala next week—"

"Not your thing?"

"The primping and the preening? God, *no*. And I don't have a dress so I have to make time to find one!"

"So, don't go to the gala," Jackson suggested on a casual shrug.

That would be first prize but impossible. "Real estate moguls can blow off important events on the town's calendar and not suffer any reprisals but, as an underpaid, almost broke cop who has been ordered to be there by her boss, I can't."

Humor flashed in his eyes again. "Is Sheriff Battle expecting violence to break out on the dance floor?"

"Funny." Hayley tipped her head up and looked at the blue Texas sky. She'd begged Nathan to let her off the hook, telling him that galas were her wealthy and socially active family's thing, not hers. She far preferred to drink a beer and shoot pool at Bert's, a bar on the outskirts of the town. Sheriff Battle listened to her impassioned plea before telling her to find a dress, get her hair done and not to be late. And if she ignored his order, she would be riding a desk for the rest of her life.

A TCC gala ball or desk duty? Both were equally tedious.

"Are you one of the first responders being honored for your work during the COVID-19 pandemic?" Jackson asked, looking curious.

Hayley sighed. At the gala ball, various first responders from fire and emergency services, as well as hospital workers, were to be inducted as honorary Texas Cattleman's Club members for their heroic service through the two worst disasters in recent Royal history—the tornado that ripped through the town in 2013 and the COVID-19 pandemic. Hayley had zero interest in joining the TCC and the idea of being lauded for doing her job made her feel deeply uncomfortable.

Hayley wrinkled her nose and refused to look at him. "I don't know who came up with that stupid idea. I was just doing my job. I don't need anyone to make a fuss." Releasing a frustrated sigh, she forced herself to meet his eyes.

"Anyway, I hope you now understand why I don't have time to waste, Mr. Michaels, so don't make me come back out here, okay?" Hayley scowled at him. "Next time I might not be quite as nice."

The smile Jackson handed her was as wide as the Texas sky above and Hayley saw the deep dimple in the left side of his cheek, and his eyes deepened to purple. His open, laughing face made her want to touch his lips with hers, to bury herself in his arms, to soak in some of his vitality and to roll around in his deep, sexy laugh.

Damn. Not good.

"This is you being nice?" Jackson asked when he stopped laughing.

Yeah, well, it had been a few tough weeks.

Jackson lifted his hand and Hayley held her breath, thinking he was about to touch her. Every hormone Hayley possessed sat up and quivered, hoping he would. But then his hand fell and he incinerated her with a hot look instead.

You're on duty, Lopez.

So?

"You need to get back to work, Harper Lopez. You need to find that baby's mama."

Hayley shook her head, a wave of tiredness and despair rolling over her. She was stumped and more than a little despondent. "I don't know if I can."

Why did she let that slip? And why in front of him, of all people? There were just a few people she opened up to and an arrogant man she met fifteen minutes before did not qualify.

Jackson cleared his throat and Hayley forced herself to look at him. All traces of amusement were gone and her breath caught at the intensity of his expression.

"You can. And you will," Jackson told her. There was no equivocation in his voice and Hayley found herself nodding, suddenly a little more energetic and optimistic.

"It's been—" he hesitated, as if looking for the right word "—interesting meeting you, Officer Lopez."

Same.

Not wanting him to leave without a solution to her Bubba problem—hell, not wanting him to leave at all— she waited until he was behind the wheel of his big-ass truck before tapping his window. He hit the button to the electric window and when it was down, she put her hand on the open window. "So, do I have your word that you will leave Bubba alone?"

Jackson flashed her another of his amazing smiles. "Not a chance, Hortense."

Hortense? Really? She sighed. "My first name is Hayley."

She wondered how long it would take him to do the computation and arrive at the right conclusion.

Five seconds passed before comprehension dawned. He was quicker than most. "Juan Lopez's only daughter? The one he's desperate to find a husband for?"

She still found it strange that everyone in town knew her father didn't approve of her moving out of the family compound—the roots of the family business were in Royal but the family relocated to Dallas over fifteen years ago—into a small apartment in town, that he was horrified at her being a cop and couldn't understand why she wouldn't stay home and play the pampered princess. He'd worked hard to give his children everything, yet his youngest and most stubborn child was determined to throw his generosity in his face.

She didn't need his generosity or his patronage. She'd make it on her own, dammit. Unlike her brothers, she refused to allow another person, even if that person was her father, to write the story of her life. She'd wield the pen, thank you very damn much.

Jackson stared at her, his expression inscrutable. "Well, that explains a lot."

He started his engine—God, it sounded good—and accelerated away.

Hayley slapped her hands on her hips and scowled at his departing truck. And what, exactly, did that mean?

So that was Hayley Lopez.

Jackson had heard of her. Few in their uber-wealthy circles didn't know about the headstrong youngest child of Juan Lopez, who'd walked away from the family to follow a career as a public servant. But he hadn't realized she was a cop or that she was so incredibly gorgeous…

Or so damn young.

Driving back to Royal, Jackson rested his wrist on top of his steering wheel and scowled into the midday sun. He'd lost his sunglasses again, the third pair this month. He was an intelligent person but keeping track of his sunglasses was beyond him. Anyone would think he was sixty-three and not thirty-six.

Thirty-six. God. Where had the years gone?

And Hayley Lopez couldn't be more than twenty-three, twenty-four? There had to be a baker's dozen years between them and that was why the thoughts he was having—what she looked like under her ugly cop uniform and whether her long hair hit her spectacular ass—were wildly inappropriate.

But there was no denying that she was hot.

With brown-black eyes that flashed fire, she had the longest eyelashes he'd ever seen and hair that was long, thick and, he suspected, a little curly. Her amazing attributes didn't stop there: cheekbones that could cut glass, a straight nose, sexy lips and a stubborn chin. And God, that body. Hayley was tall, with legs that went on forever, and on the skinny side of slim. She did, however, have amazing curves that could make lingerie models weep.

Heading back to his offices in Royal, Jackson tried to shift his attention from the sexy cop to his in-peril development but he couldn't get those flashing eyes and her obvious irritation out of his mind. Her reaction to him amused him. Most women, on meeting him socially— and it never mattered whether they were single or not— went directly into flirt mode. Hayley Lopez, probably because she had three very macho brothers and a father who took no shit, wasn't even remotely impressed by him.

Jackson wasn't sure whether to be pissed off or pleased.

Jackson heard an incoming call on his car's Bluetooth system and, scrunching his eyes up as he drove into the sun, tapped his steering wheel to answer the call.

"Michaels."

"Jackson, darling, it's Thea Bowen-Hardy."

When was he going to learn to check the display before answering calls? "Thea, I'm on another call so I can't talk."

He wasn't but he wasn't in the mood for Thea's inane conversation.

"I was wondering if you'd like to be my date for the TCC gala ball next week?" Thea asked in a breathy, baby-doll voice. No doubt about it, he far preferred Hayley Lopez's take-no-prisoners (literally, in her case) voice. "I appreciate you thinking of me—" no, he didn't "—but I already have a date."

"Ah, well, I'm sure I'll see you there."

Not if he could help it, Jackson thought as he said goodbye and disconnected the call. Thea was the last in a long line of women asking him to be their date to the TCC function. Normally he refused without an explanation so what made him tell her that he was bringing a date? And Jackson did not doubt that Thea had already texted ten of her girlfriends and her mother with the news that he, the guy who went to most functions alone—why create more chatter?—had a date for the year's most prestigious event. Jackson sighed. Knowing Royal's penchant for gossip, he'd be engaged by nightfall and married by morning.

He'd boxed himself into a corner, Jackson reluctantly admitted. If he rocked up at the gala without a date, he'd have a crapload of women pissed off at him...

He'd have to find a damn date. And that was going to be a pain in his ass. He instructed his phone to call his oldest friend and smiled when he heard her harried hello. "Why don't we have any chemistry?" he demanded.

"Hello to you, too, Jackson," Cammie drily responded. "Care to explain that out-of-the-blue statement?"

"Well, if we had chemistry, we could be married already and I wouldn't have to find a damn date for the damned gala."

Cammie laughed softly. "I'm so sorry that our lack of chemistry has inconvenienced you. Besides, I'm with Drake now and he wouldn't appreciate me ditching him to be your date."

His oldest friend had recently reconnected with her first love, Drake Rhodes, and Jackson smiled at the happiness in her voice. Cammie deserved to be loved and in love and if Drake hurt her again, he'd kick his ass. But Drake seemed to be as much in love with Cam as she was with him but he'd keep an eye on him.

Nobody was allowed to hurt the people he cared about.

"I stupidly told Thea that I had a date for the gala ball," Jackson told her, scowling when Cammie responded with a chuckle.

"You moron! You do know that she won't keep that news to herself and the world will want to know who you are taking?" Cammie asked him, pointing out the obvious.

"I'm aware," Jackson sourly replied.

"Just say yes to the next woman who asks you to the ball," she suggested.

"I'd rather shoot myself in the foot," Jackson muttered.

"Did you go out to Bubba's this morning?" Cammie asked him, changing the subject. "Is he still balking at selling?"

"He is. And Hayley Lopez is giving him legal advice, advising him of his rights and encouraging him not to sell, as if she were a real lawyer and not still studying toward her law degree," Jackson grumbled as he swung into the parking area adjacent to his office building. A lot of his colleagues found it strange that the headquarters of Michaels International, a phenomenally successful real estate development company his father started forty years ago, was based in Royal but he had satellite offices all over the world and spent most of his time on the road.

"I can't develop the area around Stone Lake without his property, so if he doesn't sell, the whole development is a nonstarter."

"Community opposition to your proposed development is growing, Jackson," Cammie told him.

Jackson cut his engine and shrugged. If he had to kowtow to the people who hated his developments, he wouldn't have built anything in the last decade. Opposition came with the territory.

He didn't march to the beat of the collective drum.

"Jackson?"

"Yeah?"

"You said you were going to call Rafe and try to persuade him to come to the gala ball. What did he say? Is he going to come?"

He'd been waiting for and dreading her question. Jackson pushed his index finger and thumb into his eye sockets, thinking of how to tell her about his and her brother's tense conversation.

It was all so damn complicated…

His father and Rafael's father had been best friends and he and Rafe grew up together. He'd watched the proud and ambitious Rafael butt heads with Tobias, partly because Tobias was demanding and controlling, partly because Rafael always felt like an outsider in his own family. He was the son of Tobias's long-term mistress and when she died, Tobias took Rafael in and gave him the Wentworth name. But his new stepmother, Cammie's mother, hated the bastard child sharing her daughter's inheritance and made his life a living hell. Jackson couldn't blame Rafe for leaving Royal but desperately wished he and Tobias could find a way back to each other.

He'd give anything to spend more time with his dad. His mom? Not so much. Jackson pushed thoughts of his family away, preferring to keep his focus on the Wentworth family. Recently he'd noticed changes in Tobias, brought on by the death of his beloved third wife, Danae. He seemed softer, less combative and abrasive. And his quiet announcement a few weeks back, telling just him and Cammie that he would be announcing, at the upcoming TCC gala, that he would fund the college expenses for all the children of the emergency service honorees, floored him.

Tobias's generosity was a side to the man he'd never expected to see. If Tobias Wentworth, proud, stubborn and ornery, could change, Jackson thought anyone could.

And maybe if Rafe saw Tobias 2.0, they'd manage to repair the Rio Grande–sized rift between them. And Cammie could have a relationship with her older brother.

So Jackson had called him yesterday, Rafe answered and Jackson asked him to attend the gala. Rafe didn't reply for the longest time before responding with a two-sentence zinger.

"My father has you as his bonus son. Does he need me there?"

That was pretty close to a no, so Jackson didn't want to give Cammie any false hope. "I don't think so, honey. I'm sorry."

Jackson heard her disappointed sigh and, wanting to change the subject, he steered Cammie away from the thorny subject of her family. "How's baby Pumpkin? I still can't believe I was out of town and missed all the excitement."

Cammie was looking after the newborn who'd been left on the hood of her car a few weeks before. The authorities—and Hayley Lopez in particular—were desperately trying to chase down his relatives.

"Good, lovely," she responded and he heard the smile in her voice. "I'm so enjoying fostering him. Did Hayley say anything about whether she was any closer to finding his mother?"

He thought back to his conversation with the firecracker, remembering her black eyes filled with fire and her kissable mouth. And body.

Too young for you, Michaels. Way too young.

"Just that she's working on it," Jackson said, exiting his vehicle. He heard the beep of another incoming call and explained that he had to go.

"It's probably another sexy single wanting to invite you to be her date for the ball," Cammie told him.

She wasn't wrong.

Two

"Morning, Mom."

Hayley, on her way out of her house, yawned and tucked her phone between her ear and her neck. Only her mom would call her shortly after first light, before she'd managed to snag a cup of coffee from the Royal Diner.

Only her mother was that brave.

"Hayley Sofia, you did not call me yesterday. How am I supposed to know that you are not dead in a ditch somewhere?" Inez demanded.

Hayley, getting into her patrol car, decided not to remind her mom that if she were hurt or missing or dead, Sheriff Nate would've called them as soon as he heard. But, since it was way too early for a fight and because she was caffeine deprived, Hayley decided to let it go. There were some arguments she would never win.

Hayley settled herself in her car and scowled at her home as she backed down her drive. Another of those no-win battles was to get her landlord to renovate the Victorian cottage she rented. Painted in shades of bright lilac and purple, it was a cookie of a house and didn't suit the tough-cop image she liked to project. But, since her landlord cut her a deal on her rent in exchange for picking up her groceries and walking her overweight bull mastiff, Peppermint, Hayley tried not to nag her.

But purple…*seriously*?

Slapping on her sunglasses, she turned right and headed into town. "How are you, Mom?"

"Fine. Your dad is fine, your brothers are fine but you, *you* don't have a date for the TCC gala!"

Oh, God, this. *Again.* Hayley turned onto Main Street and headed straight for the Royal Diner. She needed coffee, intravenously injected. Stat.

"Are you coming to the gala?" Hayley asked, trying to duck the question. "I thought you and Dad are heading for Europe next week."

"We are but Luis and Miguel will be there to represent the family and watch you get your award."

"And are Miguel and Luis bringing dates?"

"Well, no."

Ah, the usual double standard. Irritation flashed through her, as hot and as bright as a supernova. Matias was married, with kids. Luis and Miguel were still sowing acres of wild oats but Inez nagged only Hayley about her single status. It was okay for her siblings to be ambitious, to be proud, stubborn and intractable—those were traits that her parents admired but only in their boy children—but she was expected, as the baby and the girl, to be dependent. In her parents' eyes, her being ambitious meant snagging a wealthy, successful man and then producing more much-wanted grandchildren.

She was a constant disappointment, but she couldn't change for them, wouldn't change for anybody. She would never allow anyone to dictate the terms of her life, ever.

And because that was her universal truth, a cornerstone of her personality, Hayley knew that the chances of her finding a man who could love a headstrong, forthright, kick-ass-and-take-names Latina boss-girl were slim to none. Sometimes the thought made her sad, but mostly she was happy to be single, doing what she wanted when she wanted, answerable only to herself. Sure, she occasionally wished she had a pair of muscular arms to step into, a hard chest to lay her head on, a masculine mind to bounce her ideas off, but if the cost of love meant losing herself, then she'd pass, thank you.

"Chiquita..."

And that was the problem. She'd always be a little girl to her mother.

Hayley listened to her mom tell her about a distant aunt who was in the hospital having a tummy tuck—and this was important, why?—and inspected Main Street, still empty but for the occasional jogger and cyclist. The lights were on in the Royal Diner and even if it wasn't open, she knew that someone inside would give her a cup of coffee.

Hayley said goodbye to her mom and was about to pull into one of the many empty parking spaces outside the diner when she looked down the street and saw a low-slung sports car—holy shit, was that a Bugatti Chiron?—do an incredibly fast and highly illegal U-turn at the traffic light a block away.

Coffee or compliance? Hayley sighed, cursed her ability to let things go and backed out of the parking space.

If she chased the Chiron and the driver hit the accelerator, there was no way she'd be able to catch up with one of the fastest cars in the world. But it would be a stupid move for the driver as only a few people in the country owned a Chiron so she'd easily track him down.

And then she'd throw the book at him.

God, she needed coffee.

Hayley sped down East Street, flashed her lights and saw the Bugatti slow, then pull into an open space next to the RCW Steakhouse. Good deal, she thought, the driver wasn't a fool.

Getting out of her vehicle, she slowly approached the driver's door and watched as the window slid down. Damn, it was hard not to run her hand down the car's sleek body, to not feel a little envious of whoever it was who was privileged enough to drive this car-rocket. It was a masterpiece of car engineering and, yep, she was envious. God, she'd love to take it for a spin, to push it to its three-hundred-miles-per-hour top speed.

But maybe not. She wasn't sure she had the balls to go that fast.

Hayley radioed Dispatch, told them she was making a traffic stop on East and kept her eyes on the driver's hands. Nice hands, she realized, broad and masculine with long fingers and neatly clipped nails. "License and registration, please."

"Officer Lopez, you are a lovely sight first thing in the morning."

Hayley bent down to look into Texas bluebonnet eyes and sighed. Jackson Michaels. Of course it was…

"Mr. Michaels, you did a U-turn back there."

"I forgot some important papers and there wasn't a car on the road."

Ah, the old "the road was empty so the rules don't apply" argument. Hayley looked down, saw that he was holding an overlarge, Texas-size coffee mug and reminded herself that she wasn't allowed to appropriate anyone's coffee. Dammit.

Hayley stepped back as he opened the door and exited his stupidly expensive vehicle, coffee cup in his hand. She wasn't sure what to focus on, his clean-shaven face, his big body in a dark gray, Hugo Boss suit or his fabulous car.

For the first time, she wished she wasn't wearing her cop uniform, that her hair wasn't scraped back into its usual bun and that she'd remembered to swipe on some lip gloss or some mascara.

She liked her uniform, liked the authority it gave

her, but it wasn't sexy. For some asinine reason, she wanted Jackson Michaels to look at her as a woman and not as a law enforcement officer.

But a law enforcement officer she was. And would be until she passed the bar exam.

Jackson snapped his fingers in front of her face and Hayley blinked, trying to remember where she'd lost the conversation. Had she asked him for his documents yet?

"Are you still half-asleep, Hayley?"

She should tell him to call her Officer Lopez but she didn't have the energy. "I was up until about two studying and I've run out of coffee at home so I'm not firing on all cylinders yet," she admitted.

Jackson held out his mug to her. "I'm happy to share."

She shouldn't, it wasn't professional, but coffee was her happy, make-her-human juice. "You're not going to get out of a ticket by peddling my favorite drug, Michaels."

Jackson's laughter heated her from the inside out and made her lady parts sit up and pay attention. "It never occurred to me."

Liar, Hayley thought, taking his big mug. She lifted it to her mouth, tipped it and sighed when the rich, dark taste rolled over her tongue and slid down her throat. She liked her coffee sweet and rich with cream but this was black and dark. And extraordinary. She pulled it away from her mouth and looked at the cup. "Oh God, this is sensational. What is it?"

"The beans are grown on the slopes of Mount Meru

and Mount Kilimanjaro in Tanzania," Jackson replied, watching her as she sipped his coffee. He leaned back against his Chiron and crossed his ankles and his arms, looking tough and sexy and amused and sexy...all at the same time.

"You have brilliant taste in cars and coffee," Hayley told him.

"I know," he replied. He crooked his fingers in a "gimme" gesture and Hayley held his mug tight against her chest. She didn't care if it was his; possession was nine-tenths of the law.

Hayley sipped again and, eventually and reluctantly, handed him his cup back, watching as his lips hit the spot where hers had been a few seconds before. Damn, she wished that he'd kiss her. He looked like he'd be good at kissing. And sex. Very good at sex.

Jackson's grin flashed. "I would love to know what you are thinking."

Not a chance. Hayley pulled the cup from his hand, conscious that her face was a few shades hotter than it was before.

"So, how goes dress shopping?"

Hayley frowned at his out-of-left-field question. "What are you talking about?"

"A dress for the gala? You should wear red, or aqua. Jewel colors would show off your amazing skin."

He thought she had amazing skin? Really? The compliment, issued in his come-to-bed voice, made her feel alive and pretty and rather wonderful and...yes, uncomfortable. So, because she didn't know how to deal with compliments that weren't related to her work, she scowled. "Thank you, Coco Chanel."

But he was right, today was Monday, the ball was on Saturday and maybe she should make an effort to find something. She was good friends with Natalie Valentine and knew that she carried a few designer gowns at her bridal shop. "I'm hoping that Natalie will have something for me to rent."

"You're going to *hire* a dress?"

Hayley lifted one eyebrow at the horror in his voice. Jeez, she hadn't said that she was going to beat a confession out of a suspect.

"Hiring dresses is what people who can't afford designer dresses do," Hayley pointed out.

"But you're Juan Lopez's daughter."

And he assumed that she had access to Juan Lopez's credit cards and bank accounts. "I fund myself, Jackson. And I have since I was eighteen."

"I heard that you left the family fold but I, sort of, assumed that your parents still helped you out."

As did everyone else. "You assumed wrong. I don't take a cent from them…for anything."

"Why not?"

He looked genuinely perplexed but not judgmental so, instead of telling him to mind his business, Hayley decided to be truthful. "I left home after an argument with my father—"

Why was she telling him this? She never spoke to anyone about her complicated relationship with her parents.

"I told him to shove it and that I would make it on

my own, my way. So I moved to Royal, starting as a dispatcher at the station. I attended community college and saved up enough to train with the sheriff's department. I was promoted and a few years back, I started my law degree."

"All on your own?"

Hayley nodded. "All on my own." There were times when she ate ramen noodles for two weeks straight, when she slept on a blow-up mattress and nights when she came so close to calling her dad and throwing in the towel. But she was more stubborn than most and had too much pride for her good.

"In six years, I've set up a home, put myself through school, have enough for my needs." She wrinkled her nose. "But not enough to buy designer ball gowns." She tipped her head back and glared at the wide, winter sky. "If Natalie doesn't have a suitable dress for me to hire, I might just ask Sheriff Battle if I can attend in my uniform."

"And if he says no?"

Hayley shrugged. "No idea...*yet*." A plan could always be made. Hayley wrapped her hands around the still-warm coffee mug. "Are you going to the ball?"

"Mmm-hmm."

"With Cammie Wentworth?" Why was she even asking? His love life had nothing to do with her. But every cell in her body disagreed and she was one big nerve ending of overripe jealousy.

"Cammie is with Drake Rhodes," Jackson replied. "Besides, we never had any chemistry."

That was...*interesting*. Two of Royal's prettiest people with no chemistry. "Nothing?" she asked, sounding doubtful.

His lips quirked upward. "Nothing." He made an up-and-down movement, drawing attention to his ripped body. "I know, right? How can anyone resist this?"

Hayley immediately realized that he was making fun of himself. "Your lazy-ass body and ugly mug are easily resistible, Mr. Michaels." Liar, liar, pants on fire. Hayley decided to throw him a bone. "Though you do have exceptional taste in cars and coffee."

She wrinkled her nose, thinking of the ball and her mother's suggestions for a date. "So, how many women have asked you to be their date?"

One big shoulder rose and fell. "Eight? Ten? I haven't kept count."

"And why haven't you accepted? Surely there is one woman in the bunch you could tolerate for the evening."

"Sure, but I don't want to give anyone any ideas that the date might lead to something. It won't. I don't do relationships."

Hayley had no idea why his statement made her feel sad. She was overtired and, despite making inroads into his oversize mug, was undercaffeinated. That was the only reason why she was acting like a sap.

"Why not?"

"My mom, who was incredibly demanding and difficult, left when I was ten and I remember how devastated and broken my dad was. He was never the same after that. I vowed I would never put myself in a position of loving someone that much." He looked, just for a second or two, vulnerable, then embarrassed. Then his expression smoothed out. "Besides, I'm busy. I don't have time for anything that distracts me from work. I can't give a relationship the time it deserves, and I can't commit to anything other than my career."

Fair enough. She didn't have the time or inclination, either. She had a law degree to finish, a bar exam to pass, people to help. A man would only slow her down and split her priorities.

"And you? Are you going solo to the ball?"

"I'm intending to, but my mother has sent me a list of men she's already spoken to, men who would be happy to be my date," Hayley told him, sounding bitter. "I wouldn't be surprised if I opened my front door on Saturday night and found a man standing there, waiting to escort me to the TCC Clubhouse. My mother is ruthlessly efficient, and she likes getting her way."

He stared at her and Hayley tipped her head to her side, her turn to wonder what he was thinking. "What if we go together?" Jackson suggested.

Hayley slowly lowered the coffee mug. "Say what?"

"It makes sense. You need a date, I need a date but neither of us wants to find a date. We don't want to date anyone who has expectations of said date."

"I've never heard anyone use the word *date* so much in one sentence."

He waved her observation away. "C'mon, Hayley, it makes sense. It'll be a no-stress, no-pressure arrangement."

And it would get her mom off her back. Hayley thought about it, didn't see any immediate downsides and slowly nodded. "Okay."

"Excellent," Jackson said. He plucked his coffee cup from her hand and reached for the door handle of his superexpensive car. As he was about to open the door, Hayley placed her hand on his to hold the door shut. Her hand was half the size of his.

Jackson sent her a lazy smile. "As much as I'd love to stay here and shoot the breeze, I need to get to Dallas. I have an appointment I can't miss, and I need to leave now."

"Not without me giving you a ticket for your illegal U-turn."

Hayley fought to keep her face impassive, to hide her smile at his astonishment. What? Did he think she'd forgotten why she'd stopped him in the first place? Jackson shook his head, as if trying to make sense of her words. "But I gave you coffee!"

"So you *were* trying to bribe me with coffee, Mr. Michaels?" Hayley asked, tongue in cheek.

"Yes, no, yes. Shit." Jackson released the door handle and pinched the bridge of his nose. "Can you make it quick, *Officer* Lopez? I am late."

"It takes as long as it takes," Hayley told him, amused. She wandered back to her car, grabbed her book and took down his details, loving the smell of his cologne on the crisp morning air. She handed him the ticket and struggled to hold back her smile. "You're free to go. Don't get caught speeding."

Jackson folded the ticket and placed it into the inside pocket of his jacket. He ran his hand through his expertly cut hair before yanking open the door to his expensive car. He dropped into the seat and hit the start button and Hayley shivered at the sexy growl of the engine. The car turned her on. So did the man.

God help her.

"Pick me up at seven thirty on Saturday. I live in the…colorful house on Elm Street," she told him, bending down to look into his face.

"Colorful house? Can I have a bit more of a description?" Jackson asked, sounding irritated.

"You'll know it when you see it." Hayley patted the frame of his window before deliberately looking past him and frowning. As she expected, he turned his head to follow her gaze and, when he wasn't looking, she jerked the travel mug from his hand.

She grinned at him and lifted the mug in a toast. "Thanks. I'll get the mug back to you."

"What? No! Shit, Lopez! A fine and then you steal my coffee?"

Hayley turned her back to him and walked back to her patrol car, sipping his delicious brew.

Yep, when she was done drinking his truly excellent coffee, she might, maybe, be ready to face the day.

Jackson had expected to be back in Royal Tuesday afternoon but complications with his Palms Springs development had him flying east to attend a meeting with his contractor and his architect, who were arguing pretty versus practicality. Finding a solution that worked for both of them took more time than expected and after telling them to pick up the pace because the development was behind schedule, he flew back to Dallas to pick up ten garment bags that he'd carefully placed on the passenger seat of the Chiron.

Jackson steered his car down Elm Street and looked at the pretty cottages on the leafy street. It was after nine and fully dark but, so far, the houses were pretty standard, nothing he would classify as colorful. He crossed the intersection and, in his headlights, picked up a flash of purple. He drove a little farther and looked to his right, a smile stretching his lips. Her house was indeed colorful, a mixture of purple, ranging from light to dark. It was the only house on the street that could be termed *colorful*.

The house was whimsical and quirky and didn't suit his favorite, no-nonsense, can-do-it-on-my-own and don't-mess-with-me-I-carry-a-Glock cop. Still smiling, Jackson turned his head and looked left, seeing the pile of garment bags on his passenger seat. This was either going to be his best idea ever or he was going to go down in flames.

And that was why he liked Hayley. He couldn't predict how she was going to react. Yeah, she was thirteen or so years younger than him but she had the heart of a lion and the confidence of a much older woman.

He admired her independent streak and was reluctantly impressed by her determination to carve out her place in the world. He hadn't had that choice. At eighteen he'd inherited his father's huge real estate development company when his father passed away from a very unexpected heart attack. Barely an adult, he'd been faced with a hell of a choice: to sell the company for billions to a competitor and bank enough to last for several lifetimes or to take over from his dad and build on his legacy. It had been an easy decision to make and he hadn't once regretted keeping Michaels International. It was a connection to his dad, a link that death couldn't take away. Jackson also wanted to build on the great work his father had begun; he loved and admired his father and it was a privilege to pick up where he left off.

Oh, and he also freakin' loved his job.

Well, he loved it when things went well. His Stone Lake development was almost dead in the water thanks to a stubborn old man who refused to sell. After this damn ball was over, he could give the project his full attention, which probably meant arguing with Officer Lopez a lot more.

He looked forward to it.

But, tonight, he had to navigate her very tricky pride.

Picking up his phone, he pulled up her number—Bubba had given it to him after he uttered those classic words *call my lawyer*—and quickly typed a text message.

Have you found a dress yet?

Twenty seconds later, her reply hit his screen.

No. I've been busy. I'll get to it. Stop nagging.

Nagging? That was a bit harsh since he'd asked only one question. But her not finding a dress made his next task a little easier…

Open up, I'm coming in.

Jackson exited his vehicle, walked around to the passenger seat and pulled open the door. Grabbing the garment bags, he draped them over his arm and slammed the door shut before walking up the path to her shades-of-purple whimsical house. Her front door—the color of a deep, violet bruise—opened and she stood in the doorway, leaning against the doorframe.

"Those had better not be what I think they are," she told him, her eyebrows pulled into a deep scowl.

Jackson resisted dropping a kiss onto her temple, instead gently brushing past her to enter her hallway. He looked around, grateful to see that the interior was painted a warm cream, that her sofa and chairs were navy blue. There wasn't a hint of purple anywhere.

"Why on earth is your house purple?"

Hayley's eyes darted to the pile of garment bags he draped over the arm of her sofa. She shut the door behind her and Jackson took his first good look at her lovely face. Her hair tumbled over her shoulders and down her back, in beach curls just a shade short of true black. Her soft, loose sweater fell off one creamy shoulder, revealed a hot pink bra strap and draped over an amazing pair of full, high breasts. Her sweater ended at the band of her tight yoga pants, painted over her flat stomach and long, stunning legs. Damn, that ugly deputy uniform should be burned.

She looked luscious, warm and sultry and beddable. But too young, dammit. Far too young. When she was born, he was kissing Patti Smith behind the bleachers and trying to cop a feel.

God, he felt old.

"What are you doing here, Jackson?"

"I came to see you," Jackson replied, keeping his tone easy. He looked across the open-plan room to the kitchen. "Have you got any whiskey?"

Hayley rolled her eyes. "No, I don't have whiskey but I can offer you a beer. And while you're drinking it, I'll help you decide on what dress you should wear to the ball."

Jackson's eyes collided with hers. "Me?"

Hayley's smile hovered on the other side of savage. "It's the only reason I can think of for you walking into my house with a dozen or so dresses. You seem to be a smart guy and you have to know that if I won't accept help from my parents, I sure as shit won't accept it from you."

Yep, feisty. And a little exhausting. Jackson sat down on her sofa and pushed a tired hand through his hair. "I'm not looking for a fight, Lopez, so go get me that beer and we'll talk."

He saw the fire in her eyes and quickly realized his mistake. "Please will you get me a beer and I'll explain?"

"Voy a sarcale la sopa!"

Jackson watched her very nice ass walk away and

grinned. While he wasn't fluent in Spanish, he could converse and knew that she'd just uttered a slang phrase, telling him that she'd get the truth out of him. And she would. But only after he finished his beer.

"Do you want a glass?" Hayley asked him, standing in front of her old fridge. All her appliances were old. So was her furniture, but her home was lived in and colorful—rustic chic, as his decorator called it.

"It's in a glass already," Jackson told her, unable to pull his eyes off her long, lanky, sexy frame. God, what he wouldn't do to pull her down onto his lap, to slide his hand up and under her sweater, down the front of her panties. He wanted to know whether she tasted as good as he imagined, like hot sunshine, spice, whether her skin was as luscious as it looked.

He wanted her. Too damn much.

Hayley nudged his knee with the cold bottle, jerking him out of his musings. He took the bottle with a quick thanks and took a long sip, sighing as the cool liquid ran down his throat. Not wanting her to see the desire in his eyes or the action in his pants, he sat forward and looked at the open books on her coffee table, flipping the cover of one to see that it was a thick law book.

He'd hated the few law courses he'd taken at school and admired her determination to get her degree. She was the first woman he'd met who was as driven as he was but in a completely different way.

"How's it going?" he asked, genuinely interested as she sat down on the chair opposite him.

"Slowly." Hayley wrinkled her nose. "I have an assignment due on Monday and I haven't even started it yet."

"Is that why you haven't found the time to look for a dress?"

Hayley rested her bottle against her forehead. "I wish. No, I've been a little busy trying to find the parents of baby Pumpkin."

Right. The TCC gala and the abandoned baby were the favorite topics of discussion in Royal presently, with the Royal Reporters—as his friend Brett Harston called the biggest gossips—embellishing the facts to make them more salacious.

Jackson was about to ask her for an update on the case when she nodded to the pile of dresses. "You'd better not have bought those, Michaels. I'm pissed off at your highhandedness already but if you spent money on those dresses, I'm going to kick your ass, *hard*. I don't take charity from anyone."

She could try to kick his ass but he was not only taller and bigger than her—hell, he had a hundred pounds on her, easy—but he had a black belt in judo and thought he could hold his own.

"I never bought the dresses. They are—"

A hard knock on Hayley's door interrupted his explanation. Jackson frowned and looked at Hayley, who scowled. "God, I never have visitors and now I have two on the same night. It's like Grand Central Station around here."

Hayley stood up and stormed to her front door, yanking it open without checking the peephole. Hell, she was an officer of the law. Shouldn't she take a few precautions? Who knew who could be on the other side of her door, an ex-con she arrested, a dope dealer…?

"Hey, sorry to call on you so late but I have news."

Jackson stood up and looked past Hayley to see a woman standing in Hayley's hall. He took in her basic details—Caucasian, petite, long blond hair, green eyes, pretty—and realized that she was exactly the type of girl he normally dated. But, compared with Hayley's warmth and vitality, she looked a little bland, generic.

The blonde saw him, and her eyes widened in surprise. "You're Jackson Michaels."

Yeah, he knew that.

"I'm Sierra Morgan. I'm a freelance journalist working on a story for the *Royal Gazette* and *America* magazine."

"And a huge pain in my ass," Hayley said, smiling.

Sierra laughed. She turned to Jackson, her eyes bright with amusement. "Hayley and I have a love-hate relationship. I hate it that she won't share any of the details of her investigation with me and I love it when I find something she doesn't know about."

Hayley immediately tensed, her eyes bright with curiosity. "What did you find, Sierra?"

"Give me a beer and I'll tell you," Sierra retorted.

"What am I, a damn liquor store?" Hayley muttered. But she returned with a beer for Sierra, another for him, and gestured for Sierra to take the corner of the sofa, sinking to sit next to the pile of garment bags. Hayley scowled at the dresses before turning her attention back to Sierra.

"What did you find?" she asked.

Sierra nodded in Jackson's direction. "Are you happy for him to hear this?"

Hayley swiveled her neck to look at him and Jackson held his breath, wondering what she'd say. When she remained quiet, he told her that she could trust him not to repeat anything he heard. He never ran his mouth.

"He won't leave until we've had a conversation about these damn dresses," Hayley told Sierra, irritation sparking off her. "If I hear one word of this conversation on the Royal gossip line, I will disembowel you with a blunt teaspoon, Michaels."

Feisty, fierce, fabulous. Jackson ran his hand over his face and told his body to stand down. He was here to deliver some dresses, to make life a little easier for this overachiever, not to get into her head. Or into her pants.

He wanted to but he wouldn't.

Hayley sent him another "behave yourself" look and he swallowed his smile, amused that she was ballsy enough to think he'd blindly obey her dictates. He only ever did what he wanted to, when he wanted to, but for now, he'd simply listen.

Hayley sent a glance at her pile of books and frowned. He'd forgotten what it was like to try to juggle work and studying and…well, life.

"So, I have news," Sierra stated. He saw the glint of mischief in her eyes as she looked from him to Hayley. "But if I'm interrupting something I can come back tomorrow."

"You are, you're—" Hayley blushed when Sierra raised her eyebrows and Jackson found himself charmed when she waved her hands around.

"Not him," Hayley corrected. "I meant… You're interrupting my study time. And so is he. Just tell me what you found, Sierra," Hayley said.

Bending to the side, Sierra pulled a file out of her enormous tote bag and flipped open the paper cover. "These are hospital intake records for Jane Doe, who is, unfortunately, still unconscious."

Hayley's expression hardened. "How did you get those?"

Sierra pulled a face. "Let's skip that question."

"Sierra…"

Sierra sighed. "Hayley, I'm a journalist. People give me stuff they won't give to law enforcement. So, let's not look a gift horse in the mouth, okay?"

Jackson watched as Hayley, internally, debated whether to walk away or to hear Sierra out. He bet that her innate curiosity and her desire to reunite the baby with his mother would trump playing by the rules and when she gestured Sierra to continue, he realized that he'd read her correctly. Hayley had a strong moral compass but was prepared to be flexible when the occasion arose.

Good to know.

"Jane Doe was admitted the same day baby Pumpkin was found." Sierra pulled a piece of paper from the folder and handed it to Hayley. "This is the form where the patient's personal effects are recorded."

Hayley read the form and when she tensed, Jackson knew she found something of interest. "It says here that a blue-and-white-plaid handkerchief was found in a pocket of her pants."

Sierra stared at her as if waiting for her to connect the dots and it didn't take Hayley long. "It's his burp cloth."

Right, he had no idea what a burp cloth was. "What are you talking about?"

Hayley looked at him and Jackson knew that her brain was running at Mach speed. "Mothers of young babies toss it over their shoulders to protect their clothing."

Okay, got that. But he didn't understand why it was so important.

Hayley reached for her phone on the coffee table, quickly scrolling through her picture gallery. She held up a picture of a sleeping Pumpkin and Jackson noticed that the kid was wearing blue-and-white-plaid pj's and a matching cap.

"It's the same pattern as the burp cloth," Sierra said. Yep, he got that. But what did it mean?

Hayley looked from her phone to the form, her shoulders hunched. "We ruled Jane Doe out as Pumpkin's biological mother because she hasn't given birth recently. So, who is his mother and what is Jane Doe doing with this kid?"

"She could have stolen him, could have adopted him—the possibilities are endless," Sierra said, her expression troubled. "I'll nose around town in the morning and see if I can find anyone who recognizes Jane Doe. Maybe I'll get lucky."

Hayley pinned Sierra to her seat with a mock-hard

look. "Hey, sunshine, that's my job! I'm the cop, re-member?"

"It's also my job because I'm an investigative re-porter, remember?"

Hayley closed her eyes, shook her head and released a long sigh. When she opened her eyes, Jackson saw the exhaustion in her eyes and a wave of protective-ness rolled over him. She needed a solid six to eight hours of uninterrupted sleep. She also needed to slow down, to relax, to have some fun.

But he knew that Hayley would think she was slack-ing if she took even an afternoon off.

Hayley rubbed the back of her neck and when she looked at Sierra again, Jackson saw the capitulation in her eyes. "If you find out anything, anything at all, you tell me, Sierra."

"And if you find anything out, you tell me."

"That's not how this—"

Hayley's reply was interrupted by Sierra jumping to her feet. When Sierra dropped a kiss on her cheek, Hayley looked stunned at the unexpected gesture of affection.

She rubbed her cheek with the back of her hand and glared at Sierra. "What was that for?"

"You are too precious, tough girl." Sierra pulled the file from Hayley's fingers and stuffed it back in her bag. "Don't bother getting up, I'll see myself out. And Hayley?"

"Yeah?"

"Get some sleep, okay? You look like hell."

A statement he completely concurred with. She

didn't look like hell, he doubted she could, but she did need sleep. Unfortunately, he wanted Hayley to fall asleep only after he'd pleasured her. And, preferably, in his arms.

A thought that was, for a commitment-phobe, completely terrifying.

It was time to get out of here before he acted on his impulses.

He stood up and Hayley followed him to his feet, her expression inscrutable. "Where do you think you're going?"

"I agree with your friend. You need sleep."

"You're not going anywhere until you explain why there are dresses on my couch," Hayley informed him, hands on her curvy hips.

Right, the dresses; he'd forgotten about them.

"As for sleep, I can do that after I pass the bar," Hayley told him, draining her beer. "Explain the dresses, Michaels. And make it good."

Three

She had a baby's parents to find, assignments to complete, her hair to wash. But right now she had to deal with a Thor look-alike in her tiny cottage. Jackson dropped down to sit on her sofa, looking very much at home and like he belonged in her space. His big arms rested along the back, his long legs were crossed at the ankles and his eyes were deep, dark and mysterious.

And all Hayley wanted to do was to straddle those hard thighs, slam her aching core against his erection and ride herself to some mind-blowing pleasure. And, judging by the ridge in his pants, his thoughts weren't far off hers.

He wasn't her type…

Sort of.

Sure, he was gorgeous and ripped, and she wouldn't

mind exploring the wonderland that was his body, but he wasn't long-term material. And Hayley wasn't a girl who jumped into bed just to scratch an itch... Hell, she had a vibrator for that.

No, if she slept with someone it would be because she thought their attraction had legs, that he had the potential to become someone very important in her life.

Her second lover was a cowboy she adored, someone she loved enough to introduce to her folks. She'd been thinking of forever, he'd been thinking about how to access her father's bank account.

But Jackson—older and hotter—didn't want or need anything from her or, more crucially, from her family. He didn't need her family's money, their contacts or their influence. Jackson had enough of that on his own. He just seemed to dig her. And while she might be inexperienced in seduction and attraction, she knew he wanted *her*.

And that was a hell of an ego boost.

Flickers of hot, prickly attraction danced up and down her spine as heat settled between her legs. Her breasts felt achy and heavy and all the moisture in her mouth dried up...

She wanted him and if he made the smallest move— a crook of a finger, a quiet suggestion of taking her to bed—she might just agree and consequences be damned.

They could argue about the dresses later. After he rocketed her to heaven and back.

Hayley jumped when Jackson uttered a sharp curse

and watched him lean forward and start slamming her textbooks and notepads closed.

What was he doing?

"Uh—"

"I am not going to sleep with you and you're not going to study! The only place you are going is to bed. Alone."

Wow. And... What?

"You need to sleep. And I need to get out of here before I do something stupid." Jackson jammed his hands in the pockets of his pants and Hayley saw the tension in his jaw. He looked a little pissed and a lot frustrated.

Hayley felt like she was sitting in a plastic bucket on storm-tossed waves. When Jackson started stacking her books and notepads, she threw her hands up in the air. "Stop messing with my stuff, Michaels. And please tell me why you are acting like a crazy person."

Jackson stepped back and lifted his hand, leaving a small space between his thumb and forefinger. "I'm this close to losing it so don't push me, Hayley," he said, through gritted teeth.

Don't push him? What the heaving hell? "You are in my house, dumping dresses on my sofa, listening to private conversations, bossing me about and rearranging my stuff. And I'm the one who's being pushy?"

"No, you're the reason why I'm taking cold showers lately. And they haven't helped a damn!"

What was he talking ab—oh. *Oh.*

Jackson pushed both hands into his hair and tugged. "That pink bra strap is driving me nuts. I keep thinking about your amazing breasts under that silky fabric, how your ridiculously long legs would feel wrapped around my hips."

His words, uttered in that deep, sexy growl, dialed her heat factor back up to a thousand degrees. She had to be in his arms, she needed to have his lips on hers. She couldn't wait any longer to know how he tasted, whether reality came close to her imagination.

Jackson took a step back and raised his hand in a "stay there" gesture. "I'm going to go."

What? Nooooooooo! Why? Things were just getting interesting.

"I thought you were going to kiss me," Hayley whispered, shocked to hear the disappointment in her voice.

Jackson scrubbed his hands over his face. "God, I want to."

"So what's the problem?" Hayley demanded, confused.

"You're…you're…"

If she wasn't so comprehensively confused she'd be a little amused at seeing the usually confident Jackson grasping for words. "I'm…?"

"Too young!" Jackson forced the word out. "Goddammit, Hayley, I'm thirteen years older than you. You're just a kid."

What? Oh, he didn't just say that, did he? He couldn't possibly be that stupid.

"I can drink, I can vote, I can hit the bull's-eye on a target at a hundred feet away. I'm a contributing member of society, a valued member of this community. I goddamn help people every damn day! I support myself with no help from anyone." Hayley felt her voice rising with every syllable, knowing that Jackson had hit her hottest of hot buttons. She worked her ass off every day to cultivate respect, to get people to see her as capable, so Jackson's statement was a knife blow to her heart.

Angry beyond measure—angry with him because he defined her by her age and not her capability and angry with herself because she felt rejected—she pointed to her door.

"Get out!"

"Hayley—"

"Swear to God, Jackson, get the hell out of my house or I might just call for backup and make you leave." She wouldn't. She'd never tell anybody about this but he didn't need to know that.

Jackson rubbed his forehead and slowly made his way across the room. He faced her again, his expression inscrutable. "I never meant to insult you, but the fact is, I'm in my midthirties and you haven't even hit your midtwenties yet. You are still establishing your career. Mine is rock solid. You are, I think, inexperienced in bed. I am not. Yes, I'm attracted to you, you're freaking beautiful."

Blah, blah, blah…

"But we're at completely different stages in our lives, Hayley." Jackson momentarily closed his eyes. "I don't want to take advantage of you."

Take advantage? Seriously, he was talking like she had no control over her body, like someone else made the decisions about her sex and love life. Holy crap on a rocket ship, she couldn't believe this was happening.

Nobody took advantage of her, ever. She was stronger and better than that. Making her own decisions, walking her own road was the reason she bucked her father's control, rebelled against her mother's wishes. She made her own decisions and lived with the consequences of them and Jackson's making assumptions on her behalf pushed every one of her buttons.

Hayley's hot look was intended to scorch. She allowed him to see her disdain before walking past him to pull open her front door. "As I said, get the hell out of my house. And, really, don't bother picking me up on Saturday night. Despite what you think, I am a big girl and fully able to attend a TCC gala without a big, important, self-important man on my arm."

"Hayley—"

She was done. Exhausted and disappointed and on the point of tears. She refused to let him see her cry. Nobody was entitled to see her tears. Her father and brothers never had, and Jackson was barely more than a stranger.

She had work to do, assignments to complete and a baby's parents to find. That was important work. Jackson Michaels, the billionaire buffoon, was not.

"Good night, Michaels. Don't bother dropping by unannounced again."

Hayley walked away, heard the door shut behind him and closed her burning eyes. Forcing them open, she looked over her sitting room and cursed at the pile of dresses on her sofa. She looked at the door, wondering whether she had time to gather them up and get them to him, and then she heard his car start and the engine rev as he pulled away.

She'd missed her chance. Maybe that was a blessing in disguise because when she next saw Michaels again, she wanted to be ice-cold, emotionally unavailable and ridiculously formal with a badge on her waistband and a gun on her hip.

Too young, her ass.

"Hayley!"

Hayley, standing on the porch of yet another house in her quest to track down baby Pumpkin's mother, turned to watch Sierra run up the concrete path to the house, blond hair pulled into a messy knot on the top of her head. Were those wooden skewers holding her hair up?

"Why do you have chopsticks in your hair?" Hayley asked, laughing, when Sierra reached her.

Sierra grinned. "I couldn't find any hair ties and these work." She shrugged. Then she frowned. "God, you look more exhausted, if that's even possible, than you did last night."

"I already have one nagging mother, thank you very much."

Sierra sent her a naughty grin. "So, was he good in bed? He looks like he would be."

Hayley slowly lowered her sunglasses. "What the hell are you talking about?"

"Jackson Michaels, of course. Judging by the electricity crackling between you two, I kept expecting one or both of you to spontaneously combust," Sierra replied. She leaned forward. "So who jumped who? Is that grammatically correct? Should I be asking who jumped whom?"

Hayley felt the beginnings of a headache at the back of her skull. "God, you're nosy."

Sierra didn't look chastised. "I'm a reporter. It's an essential part of the job. So, did he keep you awake all night?"

"No. And that's all I'm going to say," Hayley snapped, using the side of her fist to bang on the door.

"Pity," Sierra replied. "I think you two would suit each other."

When icicles formed in hell. She'd prefer not to hook up with a guy who thought he could boss her around. She was fully independent and didn't need an alpha male making decisions for her. And if she did, her father would be at the head of that line.

Hayley sent Sierra a done-talking-about-this look. Sierra smiled and, thank God, changed the subject. "What are you doing here?"

"Door-to-door canvassing," Hayley replied, knocking on the door again. "I checked the hotels and motels a couple of weeks back but someone somewhere has to have seen Jane Doe or someone with a baby. And why isn't Mrs. Kay answering? She never goes anywhere!"

Hayley heard movement within the house and faced Sierra again. "Why are you here?"

"I was asking questions, too, and someone steered me here, told me that Mrs. Kay was renting a room to a young female. I thought I'd come and check it out."

Hayley had to admire Sierra's persistence. And

below her hardnosed reporter persona, she sensed that Sierra cared about Jane Doe and baby Pumpkin, that this was more than a story to her. She could respect that. She could even work with her, provided she didn't impede her investigation.

The door opened and Hayley smiled at Mrs. Kay, who, with her snow-white hair, curved back and deeply wrinkled face, looked like she was 104 years old.

"Hayley Lopez, how nice to see you! And you brought a friend to visit with me," Mrs. Kay said in her high-pitched squeak. "Come in, have some coffee and a slice of pie."

Hayley's mouth watered. Mrs. Kay's pecan pie had won first prize at Royal's Bake Show for ten years running and it was bliss on a plate. But she had a million things to do today and couldn't afford the time to stay and chat.

"I'm here in an official capacity, Mrs. Kay, and we can't stay for coffee. This is Sierra Morgan, by the way," Hayley explained, stepping into her overdecorated hall.

Mrs. Kay folded both hands over the knob of her wooden walking stick and looked up at Hayley with troubled eyes. "I was considering calling you, you know."

"Really? Why?" Did she want to report her cat missing again? Hayley never minded responding to Mrs. Kay's calls about her missing cat. Joseph-John had a habit of hiding out under the porch and Hayley invariably found him there, and Mrs. Kay showed her gratitude by foisting something sweet on her.

Mrs. Kay's baking was a perk of her job.

"I was wondering how long I should wait to file a missing person report."

"Who is missing, Mrs. Kay?"

Mrs. Kay shook her head and looked stubborn. "No, no… You tell me why you are here first."

Hayley nodded, resolved to return to Mrs. Kay's concerns later. "There's an unconscious woman in the hospital and we are trying to identify her. We are also trying to identify the mother of a baby left in a carrier on Cammie Wentworth's car."

"I heard about that. Bad business."

"Sierra is here because she heard that you recently rented a room to an out-of-town female," Hayley said. She lifted her phone and showed Mrs. Kay a picture of the unidentified, unconscious woman.

Recognition flared in Mrs. Kay's eyes and when Sierra tensed, Hayley knew that she saw it, too. They were on the point of a breakthrough and they both knew it.

"Will I get into trouble talking about her? Aren't there privacy laws I should be aware of?" Mrs. Kay asked, her expression troubled.

"We're trying to help her, Mrs. Kay," Hayley said, keeping her tone mellow. "Tell us what you know."

"The missing person report I thought about filing? It was for her. She paid me her rent up front, three months, but she never said anything about going anywhere and I haven't seen her in ages. But all her stuff is still in her room."

Hayley knew that Sierra was mentally doing a high

five and, to be honest, so was she. "Who is she, Mrs. Kay?"

"Her name is Eve Martin. She said she's from Miami. She had the sweetest baby boy with her."

Progress, progress, progress!

"But that's all I know," Mrs. Kay stated. "She's a lovely girl but wasn't the chatty type."

And Mrs. Kay, lonely and long widowed, loved company and would pull anyone into a conversation at any time. Hayley reminded herself to talk to the town's social worker to see if Mrs. Kay qualified for any home help or programs to get her out of her house.

"Can we see her room, Mrs. Kay?" Sierra asked.

Mrs. Kay immediately shook her head. "Well, I don't know about that. I don't think that's right."

Hayley took Mrs. Kay's old hands in hers. "You know me, Mrs. Kay. I'm trying to help her. I really am."

Mrs. Kay considered her words and quickly nodded her head. "Only because it's you and I trust you, Hayley Lopez. Let me get you the key."

When Mrs. Kay turned her back, Hayley held out her fist for Sierra to bump. They had a name for their unconscious Jane Doe and a probable connection to baby Pumpkin. Awesome news.

After searching the room, Hayley and Sierra decamped to Hayley's house to examine various items of interest they'd found in Eve's room.

Hayley led Sierra into her living room and scowled at the pile of dresses still sitting on her sofa. She needed to do something about them…

No, Jackson had brought them over without asking her. It was his job to take them away. Hayley told Sierra to take a seat and, after dropping Eve's bagged and tagged personal obsessions onto her coffee table, pulled up Jackson's phone number.

Typing quickly, she told him that she was home and that he needed to pick up the dresses. If they weren't out of her house by that evening, she'd donate them to the charity shop downtown.

Jackson's reply hit her phone ten seconds later.

Do you have a dress yet? Of course you don't, so for God's sake, pick one! And, no, I didn't buy them. A friend of mine owns a dress shop in Dallas and she's happy to take everything back.

Not being a child. I can find, and buy, my own dresses. Get them out of here by 5:00 p.m.

Hayley tossed her device onto the coffee table and slapped her hands on her hips. "Men. Can't deal with them, can't shoot them."

"Jackson Michaels?"

"Who else? And no, I don't want to talk about it," Hayley snapped. Wincing, she sent Sierra an apologetic look. "Sorry. Do you want coffee or something?"

Sierra shook her head. "No, thanks. I just want to look at her stuff." Sierra nodded to the evidence bags on the table.

Hayley looked up at the ceiling, looking uncomfortable. "We shouldn't be looking at any of this. We have no right to it and I will be taking it back to Jane Doe in the morning."

"We can have a quick peek, surely?"

"I'm just looking at her stuff so that I can find out who she is," Hayley told Sierra, thinking of the fine line between respecting Jane Doe's privacy and investigating. "I'm just gathering information."

Hayley opened a bag and pulled out Eve's ID, her eyes drifting over her fine features.

Who are you, Eve Martin? All she knew so far was her name and that she was twenty-eight and from Miami.

Miami was a city of close to half a million residents. Why couldn't she be from a small, Podunk town of five hundred?

Sierra pulled out a book covered in leather. She flipped it open and, glancing at it, Hayley saw the feminine writing. Was Sierra holding Eve's diary? If she was, then score! Diaries were great sources of information.

She wouldn't read it but Sierra could. Nobody, as far as she knew, had committed a crime so it wasn't evidence…

"What does Eve have to say? Does she mention the baby?" Hayley demanded.

Sierra shook her head, her eyes moving across the page. She flipped a page, then another and eventually looked up, her eyes puzzled. "This isn't Eve's diary, but her sister's, I think. She talks about Eve in the third person and…holy crap."

Hayley almost had to sit on her hands to stop herself from yanking the diary out of Sierra's hands. "What?"

"The baby's name is Micah. He is her sister's son."

Hayley took a moment to process that information. "Does it say why Eve has the baby?"

Sierra shook her head. "Not that I can see."

"Any mention of the baby's father?"

"Again, not at first glance." Sierra frowned at her. "Are you wanting to reunite the baby and his father?"

Hayley lifted one shoulder in a shrug. "I'd like to, at the very least, establish who the father is so that I can contact him. He might be going crazy wondering where they are, what's happened to them."

"Or he might not even know of the existence of a child," Sierra pointed out.

Fair point. "I'll need to head back to the station, see if anyone has reported Eve Martin or baby Micah missing. I'll also run a check and see if I can pull up details on who her sister is."

Sierra held the book up so that Hayley could see the front inside cover and the first page. Arielle Martin, Miami, 2020.

Well, then. That helped.

Hayley stood up and smiled as Sierra toed off her sneakers and lifted her feet, covered in bright red socks, onto her sofa, her nose buried in Arielle's diary. Hayley knew it was important that they discover who Arielle and Eve were but found reading the private thoughts of another woman disconcerting. But it was necessary and Sierra didn't seem to have any qualms so Hayley would leave her to it.

"Help yourself to whatever you need," Hayley told her, picking up her phone. "Call me if you find anything interesting."

"I've found something interesting," Sierra stated, just as Hayley was about to open her front door.

Walking back into the sitting room, Hayley stood in front of her. "What?"

"There is one mention of Micah's father," Sierra said, finally lifting her eyes from the book.

"Well, who is it?" Hayley impatiently demanded.

"There isn't a name." Of course there wasn't. That would be too easy. "But she writes that he's from Royal and, drumroll, please..."

She was fond of Sierra but it had been a long day and she wasn't in the mood for games. "Sierra," Hayley warned.

"She says that he's a member of the Texas Cattleman's Club."

"Marvelous," Hayley sourly stated. "The TCC members are only the most influential, richest, boldest and most powerful men in the country, maybe even the world."

"But that's what makes it interesting. And fun." Sierra smiled at her, her expression impish. "I like ruffling feathers."

Hayley had noticed. Sierra was a bit like a large wave. Sometimes it was easier to go with the flow than fight it.

"Huh, that's strange."

Sierra held up the diary to show Hayley an almost blank page except for a name—Rafael Wentworth—

bracketed by several asterisks. Cammie's brother? Rafael was the black sheep of the Wentworth family... Could he also be baby Micah's father?

"I need to start at the beginning and work through the diary systematically, making notes as I go," Sierra stated before placing the diary on the cushion next to her. She looked to her right at the pile of garment bags on that end of the sofa. "As we've already established, I'm incredibly nosy... Can I take a look?"

Hayley shrugged. "Knock yourself out. Jackson Michaels brought them over.

"He probably wanted to make sure I didn't embarrass him at the TCC gala," she added, her tone bitter.

"You're going to the gala with him?" Sierra asked, standing up.

"I *was* going with him. Now I'd rather stick hot coals under my tongue."

Sierra pulled down the zip of a bag and pulled out a soft gray ball gown. Pretty but a little dull. "What did he do?"

Hayley had a lot of friends but no one she was close to and, inexplicably, she needed to talk, to get someone else's perspective on last night's suck fest. "We have this weird attraction. All I can think about is jumping him. And I know he's attracted to me, too, but—"

Sierra opened another bag, saw the pink frothy material and immediately zipped the bag up again. Good call. She wouldn't be seen dead in anything that color. "But?"

"I, kinda, suggested that he should kiss me and

he, explicitly, told me he wanted to but that I was too young."

Sierra frowned at that. "But you're in your late twenties, aren't you?"

Because of her height, people always assumed she was older than she looked. "I'm turning twenty-four in a few months."

"You're twenty-three? But you're so damn mature and together," Sierra spluttered, looking a little confused. She pulled out a red dress, laid it on the couch and slowly nodded. "I like it."

"I'm not wearing any of those dresses. They are going back to him, unused. I am not his charity case."

"Mature, together and very stubborn. And young," Sierra added.

Hayley threw up her hands. "I can't help my age, Sierra!"

"I know that, honey, but he is thirteen or so years older than you. And what would you prefer...a guy who takes what's on offer without a thought to the age and power dynamic between you or a guy thoughtful enough to consider the dynamics and the consequences of you hopping into bed together?"

Well, when she put it like that. "It's my body, I am fully able to decide if I want sex or not," Hayley muttered. "It's not like I asked him to marry me."

"Of course you are," Sierra told her. "And of course you didn't. But, as your friend, and we are on our way to being good friends, Hayley Lopez, I am happy to know that Jackson isn't the type to rush in and take advantage of someone a lot younger than him."

"He wouldn't be taking advantage. I want to sleep with him!" Hayley shouted, frustrated.

"Good to know."

Oh, Jesus, oh no. Crap. Hayley spun around, praying that she'd imagined his voice, that she was starting to hear crazy voices in her head and having delusions because anything would be better than having to face Jackson Michaels ten seconds after *that* heated declaration.

Sierra held her stomach, tears of laughter streaming down her face. Hayley glared at her and raised her index finger. "You know what you said about us being friends? Not gonna happen."

"Nah, it will," Sierra told her between laughter-tinged hiccups. She held up a silver dress and Hayley's breath caught somewhere in her throat. Despite feeling Jackson coming up to stand behind her, smelling his cologne and feeling his heat, her attention was snagged by the panels of fine silver silk. The neckline of the dress would end halfway to her navel, and the spaghetti straps were anchored to the draping fabric at the sides. The back would skim her butt and the color suited her complexion.

Yeah, she could work with the dress.

Straightening her spine, she lifted her chin, hoping her face wasn't still on fire. "I'm going back to the station." She pointed at Sierra again. "Go through the diary, let me know if you find anything."

Hayley turned to Jackson and lifted her eyes, slamming into all that purple-blue. There was amusement in those dark depths but she also caught a hint of remorse. He opened his mouth to speak but Hayley cut him off.

"Get those dresses out of here. But leave the silver one. I might—or might not—wear it. Text me the details of your friend in Dallas so that I can talk to her about buying it—" She saw him about to speak, knew that he was considering buying it for her and handed him a hard look that said don't even go there. Jackson's mouth snapped closed and she nodded. "Pick me up on Saturday night unless…"

She stopped talking and deliberately waited for him to prompt her to continue. "Unless?"

"Unless I'm too much for an old man like you to handle."

Jackson's mouth fell open, either at her insult to his age or the challenge, but she didn't care. He was caught off guard and that was the way she liked him. The man was far too confident and self-assured.

On Saturday night she'd blow all thoughts of their age difference out the window and they'd see exactly who could resist whom.

Guaranteed, she wouldn't be the one begging for a kiss when the night ended.

Four

Hayley had lived and worked in Royal for years and Jackson never noticed her before. But on this Friday morning, the day before the gala, she seemed to be everywhere. He'd seen her patrol car pass his offices when he walked into his building shortly before seven this morning, caught a glimpse of her talking to Sheriff Nate Battle on the steps of the courthouse earlier and now she was interrupting his lunch with Brett Harston and Clint Rockwell, old friends and fellow TCC members. To be fair, she wasn't interrupting per se— he was seated in a booth and she was standing at the counter ordering lunch to go—but she was the reason he'd lost track of the conversation.

When Hayley was around, hell, even when she wasn't, she tended to dominate his thoughts. And that had to stop. There were a hundred reasons why he shouldn't be thinking about her but the top three were that she was too young, too headstrong and too much of a handful.

He didn't have the time, energy or inclination to become emotionally involved, wrapped up in a woman, *any* woman. Even if he wasn't gun-shy after watching his mother make his father's life hell, he had a multibillion-dollar business to run, deals to strike, developments to build. His business required his time and focus and he owed it to his dad to carry on his good work and legacy. He just needed to get through tomorrow night and he and Officer Lopez could go back to being polite strangers.

He'd pick her up, escort her to the ball, be polite and then he'd drop her off and...

Leave.

"He wouldn't be taking advantage. I want to sleep with him!"

Her words reverberated in his head and Jackson sighed, telling himself for the billionth time that he could not take her up on her offer, that sleeping with her wasn't going to happen.

Too young, too headstrong, too unforgettable...

Brett snapped his fingers in front of Jackson's face. He jerked his eyes off Hayley's butt and back to his friend's face. He far preferred looking at Hayley; she was a lot prettier.

"Yeah, I heard that you are taking Officer Lopez to the gala," Brett stated, raising one eyebrow.

Jackson bristled. "So? Her parents wanted to choose her partner and every single woman in Dallas and

Royal wanted me to be their date so it was a mutually beneficial arrangement."

"Every single woman? Exaggerating much, Jack?" Clint asked, amused.

Jackson, discreetly, lifted his middle finger. "You know what I mean… Hayley and me, it's an *arrangement*, not a date."

"Really?" Brett mocked him, "An arrangement? Do you always bring a dozen dresses back from Dallas for a business arrangement?"

Jackson released a long groan. "Where did you hear that?"

Brett shrugged. "Dude, the Royal Reporters are on fire and you know that you are one of their favorite topics of conversation."

"Any way to shut them up?" Jackson asked, knowing it was a stupid question. Gossip was Royal's much-loved pastime.

"Get married," Clint suggested.

Jackson scowled. "Very funny, Rockwell." He'd rather put his head in a gas oven.

"Actually, it was a serious suggestion. Being happily married is a firewall between you and the gossips. The RRs don't find married bliss very interesting."

To be fair, it was a good point. Since their marriages, neither Brett nor Clint was the subject of gossip. Besides, he didn't care what people said about him. He was rich and powerful enough for that not to matter.

On the other hand, Hayley wasn't. She was a public servant, someone who needed the community's trust to work effectively. She'd hate being gossiped about…

And maybe he should have thought about that before he asked her to be his date to the ball, before he brought those dresses back from Dallas. Thanks to his wealth and power, he was insulated but she didn't need the town commenting on her life.

Jackson gestured the waitress over, asked her to fill his mug and looked across the table to his friends. "Officer Lopez is run off her feet trying to reunite the abandoned baby with his mother, and she has no time to go dress shopping. She heard I was going to Dallas and asked me to collect the dresses. Hell, if she had her way, she would go to the gala in her uniform."

Jackson gestured to the waitress to fill up his friends' mugs, as well. "I might walk in with her tomorrow, but after that, we'll go our separate ways. It isn't a date," he added, conscious of the server's flapping ears.

The waitress stepped back and Jackson smiled at her. "Thanks, Cathy."

Cathy left and Brett nodded, looking impressed. "Way to quash the rumors, dude. Your words, twisted and turned, will be all over town in—" he looked at his watch "—two hours."

Jackson looked at Hayley, his eyes drifting down her slim back. "She doesn't need to be talked about," Jackson muttered.

"Well, then I suggest that you take her eyes off her ass and stop drooling," Clint suggested.

Jackson immediately wiped his mouth with the back of his hand. His hand came away dry and he glared at Clint. "Not funny, dude."

"Actually, it was."

"Yeah, it was," Brett agreed, laughing. He looked at Clint and waggled his eyebrows. "Are you buying his early declaration that she's an arrangement, not a date?"

"Not even a little bit."

Jackson pushed his coffee cup away and tossed some bills on the table to cover his share of lunch. "I'm not looking to put a noose around my neck and she's way too young for me."

"Sarabeth is ten years older than me and it's not an issue," Brett pointed out. "It's not like Hayley is desperate to please. She's super smart, driven, community-minded and mature."

Clint sipped his coffee and nodded. "What he said."

"What is it with married people and their need to see everyone around them in front of a preacher?" Jackson demanded, standing up.

Clint shrugged and smiled. "We've found the one person we want to irritate for the rest of our lives. We want that for you, too."

His back to the room, Jackson raised his middle finger again and walked away to the sound of his friends' laughter. Assholes.

Leaving the restaurant, Jackson saw Hayley's squad car parked on the opposite side of the road. He shouldn't, it would cause more talk, but his feet refused to obey his brain's command.

Jackson crossed over and saw that she was steadily making her way through a huge helping of pesto-and-pasta salad.

"Hungry?" he asked, bending down to look into the open car window.

Hayley yelped and her fork wobbled and pieces of pasta landed on her shirt. Cursing him, she grabbed a napkin and cleaned herself up.

"Do not sneak up on me, Michaels."

"Shouldn't you be more aware of your surroundings?" Jackson asked her. "What if I were a meth head or a mugger?"

"Yeah, we see a lot of those in Royal," Hayley snorted as she snapped the lid onto the container. Her lovely brow furrowed and she wrinkled her nose. "Actually, we did bust up that meth lab a few months back and Candice Johns was mugged a few years ago." After placing the lid onto her salad container, she wiped her fingers and looked at him with eyes that held a touch of frost. "What do you want, Michaels?"

Her naked, her long legs around his hips or over his shoulders, his mouth on her… God, he had to pull himself together. "Seven thirty tomorrow?"

"I thought we already agreed on that," Hayley said, not letting him off the hook.

Jackson rubbed the back of his neck, amazed at her ability to cut through his bullshit. "Yeah, we had."

"So… What's the real reason you crossed the street to talk to me?" Hayley demanded.

"God knows," Jackson testily replied. "You drive me nuts. You know that, right?"

Hayley's grin was unexpected and as bright as the sun. "Yay, because you drive me nuts, too. Good thing that we won't see much of each other after tomorrow night, right?"

Yeah, it was a good thing. An excellent thing. Then why did his heart hurt at the thought?

Their eyes, brown and blue, connected and held and Jackson felt himself spinning down a vortex. He reached out to grab the window of her vehicle, trying to ignore the thought that these were the eyes he'd been waiting for, the face he could look at for the longest time, the body he needed to make his own.

He wanted her. A little less than he didn't want to want her.

"I should go," Hayley said, her voice soft and sounding, uncharacteristically, confused. She waved her hand at the notebook lying on the passenger seat. "I need to get to the hospital."

The mention of the hospital had the hair on the back of his neck lifting. "Are you okay? Why are you going to the hospital? Who are you going to see there?"

A slow, sexy smile lifted the corners of Hayley's mouth. "Why, worried that you might have to find another date for tomorrow night?"

Jackson did a mental eye roll. If only his life was that simple. "Explanation, Lopez. Now."

Hayley didn't look impressed at his command. "Not that it has anything to do with you, but I have to interview Jane Doe. I got word that she regained consciousness a few hours ago."

A troubled expression crossed her face and he wanted to wade into her life, sword swinging and mowing down anyone and anything that caused her a moment of stress and tension. *Overreacting much, dude?*

And Hayley was the last woman who wanted, or needed, the white-knight approach. Jackson opened her door and dropped to his haunches, resting his arm on his bent knee. *Can your savior impulse and see if you can help, moron.*

"Can you tell me or is it sheriff's department business?"

"It's official business," Hayley told him, her eyes on his face.

Damn, that was the answer he expected.

"But—" Hayley said as he started to rise. Jackson immediately resumed his position, prepared to listen to anything she was prepared to tell him.

"But I, for some strange reason, trust you to keep your mouth shut. I shouldn't but I do and I need—"

She stopped talking and Jackson wanted to howl. What did she need, how could he help her? He resisted the impulse to demand that she carry on speaking and, reining in his impatience, waited her out.

"I know her name, her real name. It's Eve Martin. I did a background check on her. She's from Miami and she's a suspect in a case down there."

"What did she do?"

"She, *allegedly*, embezzled a ton of cash from the investment bank she worked at."

"Are you heading over there to arrest her?"

Hayley shook her head. "The Miami PD are still building their case so no arrest warrant has been issued yet. No, I'm just going over there to talk to her."

Jackson placed his hand on her knee. "That sounds pretty straightforward, so what's worrying you?"

Hayley's slim shoulders reached her ears and confusion skittered across her face. "I just feel like… I have this intense…*crap*."

"Just spit it out, Lopez."

Hayley stared at his fingers on her knee. "It's silly, I'm just being weird."

"Let me be the judge of that," Jackson gently suggested, squeezing her knee.

Hayley hauled in a deep breath and for a moment, a quick flash, she looked a little lost and so very damn… young.

"I'm about to sound stupid and I hate sounding stupid."

Of course she did. Jackson smiled. "At the risk of repeating myself, let me be the judge of that, sweetheart."

Hayley looked like she was going to object to his endearment but caught her words on her tongue. She rested her head against the headrest, her eyes on his. "My *abuela*, my mother's grandmother—not the one who owned a cabin next to Bubba—"

Whoa, hold on. "Your grandmother owned a cabin on Stone Lake?"

Hayley nodded. "The Lopez empire started in Royal. Didn't you know that?"

He did not.

"I loved that house, loved spending time with my grandparents on the lake. It's another reason why I'll fight to keep it the way it is."

Damn, she was emotionally attached to the lake.

It held memories that she didn't want to be tainted. From experience, he knew that the hardest people to sway were the ones who had a visceral attachment to the land.

But Jackson thought he had some valid reasons for developing the land. He'd yet to do a project in Royal, and he wanted something he could put his dad's name to. His projects provided jobs, stimulated the local economy and boosted municipal coffers. All things his dad approved of.

But he wasn't going to argue with her about the development now. "Tell me why you are feeling angsty," Jackson reminded her.

"Right. Well, my *abuela* had this uncanny ability to see into the future, to know when stuff was heading her way. She said that she felt like she was standing on the edge of a chasm, about to fall. The feeling of wanting to look over your shoulder, like you are waiting for the hammer to drop on your head."

"And you are feeling like that?"

Another shrug. "Sort of. I feel like I am setting in motion something that is uncontrollable, something that has repercussions."

"Are you talking about your professional or private life?"

Hayley lifted both shoulders to her ears. "I'm not sure…either? Both?

"I live an unexciting life, Jackson. I work and I study," Hayley added. "Occasionally, I talk to the less privileged about their legal rights, but always with the disclaimer that I'm not a qualified lawyer. But between

Eve Martin, the abandoned baby, being an honoree at this damn gala and my sudden and ridiculously inconvenient attraction to you, I feel like I'm sitting in a leaking boat on a stormy ocean. I'm feeling…"

"What, sweetheart?"

This time, she didn't react to his endearment. Progress, Jackson thought.

"Overwhelmed," Hayley admitted. "And I hate feeling like that! It's not who I am. I control my thoughts and feelings, not the other way around."

He remembered being her age, remembered thinking that as he was now an adult, he had to have everything figured out. But life was a constantly evolving process and once you have a handle on one thing, a dozen other issues always bubbled up to challenge your confidence.

"Hayley, take a deep breath. You don't have to have a handle on everything all the time. Just focus on what's directly in front of you, tackle that, and then move on to the next thing. You'll work out the rest."

"Promise?"

Jackson stood up and handed her a reassuring smile. "Go to work, tough girl." He saw the hesitation in her eyes and nodded. "You can trust me to keep anything you say confidential, Hayley."

Fire flashed in her eyes again. "If you don't, I'll just arrest you for obstructing an investigation."

He grinned, happy to see that she was back to being fierce. He tapped the roof of her car and stepped back. "Go to work, Officer Lopez. And I'll see you tomorrow night."

Hayley wrinkled her nose. "Schmoozing and smiling. I'm not looking forward to it at all."

She started the engine of her car and pulled off into the traffic. Thank God he had a fairly healthy ego or she would've destroyed *his* confidence several conversations ago.

Hayley walked into the Royal Memorial Hospital and headed toward the bank of elevators, jabbing the button with her free hand. Lifting her bottle of water, she sipped and considered the conundrum that was Jackson Michaels.

He was a tough and ruthless businessman, bossy as hell, but—for reasons she couldn't yet pinpoint—she trusted him.

And Hayley didn't trust easily.

Hayley stepped into the elevator and pushed the button for the third floor, happy for a few minutes alone to gather her thoughts. Maybe she found it easy to speak to Jackson because he was wholly unconnected to her day-to-day life. As one of the few women in law enforcement in Royal, she had to work twice as hard as her male counterparts and not give them any excuse to see her as weak or emotional or temperamental. She couldn't talk to her family because if she even hinted at any dissatisfaction with her situation—work or otherwise—they would use her words against her, insisting that she come home, get married, play it safe.

Like Sierra, Jackson didn't seem bothered by her smart mouth or independent streak, and when she was around him, she felt like she'd found her safe space, the place where she could be herself.

Why him and why now? He was a lot older than she was but that didn't bother her in the least. She could handle him…

But only when they were fully clothed.

He'd take control in the bedroom, of that Hayley had no doubt. He'd push her to explore her sexuality, to try new ways of making love, would introduce her to new positions, push her out of her comfort zone. *Comfort zone? You have to have a love life to have a zone, Lopez!*

Anyway, Jackson would be a demanding lover, someone who expected his partner to keep up with him. She wished she could say that she was sexually adventurous, but the truth was that she wasn't. At all.

She wasn't a virgin but she'd slept with only two guys. She'd taken her first lover to assuage her curiosity— and the entire act had been a disappointment of epic proportions. Her second foray into sex had been a bit better—no fireworks but better than blah. She'd taken him home, introduced him around, invited him to move in. One morning, after falling asleep with her head on her cowboy's chest, she'd woken up to an empty apartment and a note telling her he was out of there because her father refused to invest in his cowboy-themed bar.

Oh, and that he was going back to his wife.

His wife… *Dios.*

After that debacle—and months of sleepless nights worrying that she'd be cited as the other woman in a divorce settlement—she'd taken herself off the market and devoted her time and energy to her job and her studies.

But Jackson Michaels, older, hotter and experienced, was the first man in years who had her imagining what his body looked like under his designer clothes. She wanted to know whether his skin tasted a little salty on her tongue, to rim her tongue around his belly button and over his hard abs, to push her fingernails into his gorgeous ass.

She wanted him…

Dammit.

"Ma'am?"

Hayley blinked, realized that she'd reached her floor and that the elevator doors were open and a group of people were waiting for her to leave the space. Hayley strode out of the elevator, apologized and tossed her empty water bottle in a recycling container on her way to the nurses' desk.

Eve Martin had been moved to a private room and Hayley followed the nurse inside. Eve was asleep and Hayley moved to a position just out of the patient's eyesight and leaned her shoulder into the wall, taking a minute to inspect the woman who was at the center of her case.

With her golden-brown skin and long brown hair, she was beautiful, her Afro-Caribbean roots easy to see. Long eyelashes rested against her skin and her cheekbones were high and full.

But criminals could be beautiful, Hayley reminded herself. Monsters sometimes came in pretty packaging. It was her job to be cynical, to be unemotional, to find the truth.

The nurse woke Eve up, helped her sit up and took her blood pressure and her temperature.

When she was done, the nurse gestured to Hayley, who stepped forward. "Officer Lopez would like to talk to you."

Eve whipped her head around and big eyes, scared eyes, slammed into hers. "Are you here to arrest me? Where's Micah?" She immediately tried to get out of bed, reaching for her IV drip to yank it out of her arm.

Ah, confirmation! "Micah is safe," Hayley quickly told Eve as the nurse slapped her hand over Eve's to stop her from pulling out the needle.

"You regained consciousness a few hours ago, Ms. Martin, and you're not going anywhere," the nurse told Eve in a don't-try-me voice.

Eve looked at Hayley again. "Are you sure he's okay?"

"He is. He is staying with foster parents Cammie Wentworth and her fiancé, Drake Rhodes. They are good people. They didn't know his name, so they've been calling him Pumpkin."

"Can I see him?"

Hardening her heart against the hope in Eve's eyes, Hayley sat down in a visitor's chair and pulled her notebook out of her bag. "Let's get through this interview and then we can discuss your access to the baby."

Worry flashed in Eve's eyes and she pulled her bottom lip between her teeth. "What do you want to know?"

There was so much to discuss, and Hayley wondered where to start. Because she believed that you caught more bees with honey than with vinegar, she crossed her legs and leaned back in her chair.

"Tell me about yourself—what you do, where you are from."

"My name is Eve Martin, but I guess you know that already."

Hayley didn't respond and waited for Eve to continue. She picked up a glass of water, took a sip, and Hayley tried to hide her impatience. Eve replaced the glass and was about to speak when a knock on the door distracted her.

Hayley whirled around and rolled her eyes when she saw Sierra's face between the door and the frame. "Can I come in?" Sierra asked.

"I'm conducting an interview, Morgan," Hayley grumbled.

Sierra ignored her and walked over to Eve, her expression gentle. "Hi there, I'm Sierra. I'm an investigative journalist and your story has me intrigued. How are you doing?"

Eve simply shrugged and Sierra perched on the side of her bed. "You scared us," she told the wan patient.

"I scared me, too," Eve admitted.

"What happened?" Sierra asked.

It was a question Hayley wanted the answer to, so she decided to wait to kick Sierra out. "That's a long story," Eve said, sounding exhausted.

"And one we're both eager to hear," Sierra replied. "I've been helping Hayley with her investigation."

"Journalists don't help cops, Morgan," Hayley reminded her. Again. She turned to Eve. "I can make her leave if you want to keep this discussion confidential, Ms. Martin."

"Call me Eve and I've got nothing to hide so she can stay," Eve replied.

Okay, then.

Sierra left the bed, pulled up another chair and sat down. "We're listening, Eve."

Eve looked at Hayley. "So, I guess you know that I'm under investigation for embezzlement."

Hayley nodded.

"I'm surprised I haven't been cuffed to the bed."

"Miami PD hasn't issued an arrest warrant yet," Hayley explained.

"I'm being framed."

That's what they all said, Hayley thought.

Eve pushed her hair off her forehead. "I have an affinity for finance and numbers. Not to brag, but I've been called brilliant. I've been working as an assistant analyst in an investment bank in Miami and because my boss is a slacker, and because I'm good at crunching numbers and spotting trends, my boss entrusted me with passwords and account access."

That was the how. Now she needed the why, Hayley thought.

"Along with another analyst, I was up for promotion and I think she set me up to get me out of the promotion race. She's the type who would stab you in the back and climb over your still-writhing body on her way to the top. She did a damn good job of convincing the powers that be that I'm a thief. The bank laid a charge, I'm being investigated and they got a court order to freeze my bank accounts."

Wow, they weren't playing games, Hayley thought, making a note.

Eve stared at the wall beyond Sierra's shoulder, her thoughts miles away. "My life collapsed around me. Just a few days before I was framed, I received news of my sister's death. I was shocked and devastated. I wasn't surprised to hear that she'd named me as guardian of her son, Micah. I'm the only family she has... had. I watched Micah being born and now I have to raise him."

She released a tiny sob. "Do you know how much babies need and how difficult it is to buy stuff when most of your money is tied up in a frozen bank account?"

"Most of your money?" Hayley asked, picking up the nuanced phrase.

"I had money I kept at home," Eve admitted. "My grandmother gave me ten thousand in cash before she died and made me promise I wouldn't bank it. She hated banks."

A good move, as it turned out.

"What happened to your sister?" Sierra asked.

"She died of a heart attack," Eve replied, rubbing her hands over her face. When she lowered them, Hayley saw the distress and grief in her eyes. She was either a damn good actress or innocent. Time would tell.

But Hayley was leaning toward innocent; there was too much emotion swirling in her eyes to be faked. This woman had been through a lot, losing her sister, her only family. Hayley was frequently at odds with her family but they were all healthy, thank God.

Healthy, wealthy and successful. She had a lot to be grateful for.

"I collected Micah and met with a lawyer who said it looked bad for me, that the evidence against me was strong." Eve's tormented eyes met Hayley's. "I was scared to the depths of my soul. I took a good hard look at the crappy situation I was in and decided my only option was to run."

"Why?" Sierra demanded, leaning forward. "Why run? Running makes you look guilty."

"I was facing immediate arrest and I knew the moment I was arrested, Micah would be tossed into the system and I wasn't going to let that happen. So I packed a backpack for me and one for the baby and hopped on a Greyhound bus and headed here, to Royal."

"Why Royal?" Hayley asked.

Eve pulled her bottom lip between her thumb and index finger. "I found my sister's diary. It was in Micah's diaper bag. I read it because I needed information on Micah's father. I still don't understand why she wouldn't tell me who he is. She told me everything!"

Hayley exchanged a look with Sierra. Now they were getting somewhere. "Carry on, Eve."

"Yeah, you're doing great," Sierra told her, with an encouraging smile.

Good reporter, bad cop, Hayley thought.

"Arielle didn't name names, but she did imply that

Micah's father is from Royal and that he has some connection to the Texas Cattleman's Club."

What was wrong with just writing down his name? Why did Arielle have to be cryptic about Micah's parentage? Were these people trying to make her job harder?

"What did Arielle do for work?" Sierra asked and Hayley admitted it was a good question.

"She was a photojournalist. She was really good," Eve wistfully replied. "Before she returned to Miami to have Micah, she traveled around and took odd jobs looking for interesting small-town tales."

"Her diary was mostly focused on her time in Royal, Texas, and a 110-year-old story with ties to the powerful TCC," Sierra said, looking down at her notebook.

Hayley waited for Sierra to look at her and when she did, she raised her eyebrows. This was information she hadn't yet heard and Hayley wanted to know why.

"I was going to tell you, I swear," Sierra told her, not at all chastised. She looked at Eve and shrugged. "I've been reading Arielle's diary, mostly to figure out who you, and Micah, are. But I am equally fascinated by the century-old mystery Arielle mentioned."

Eve smiled wanly. "She told me about it and I'm equally fascinated."

"It would help if I knew what you two were talking about," Hayley told them, too tired to use her scary-cop voice. It wouldn't work on Sierra anyway.

Eve looked at Sierra. "I'm tired. Would you mind explaining?"

Sierra stood up and started to pace the room. "Arielle, Eve's sister, worked as an aide in Royal's assisted living center and was transfixed by Harmon Wentworth's story."

"Is he related to Tobias Wentworth?" Hayley asked.

"A second cousin. Harmon was a hundred years old and he told Arielle a secret he'd never divulged before. Apparently, he was adopted and he always wondered who his birth mother was."

Eve picked up the story. "He was left on a doorstep in Royal, Texas, one hundred years ago without a note. Arielle's diary reveals that the long-ago baby was somehow connected to a feud between the Langley and Wentworth families at the time of the TCC's founding."

Okay, this was all very interesting, but all this happened a long time ago and Hayley had to deal with the here and now.

"We're getting sidetracked," Hayley told them. She looked at Eve and raised her eyebrows. "I need to know why you left Micah on the hood of a car in the middle of a hospital parking lot."

Eve's eyes held the sheen of unshed tears. "Not my finest moment."

Sierra was about to jump in and reassure Eve but Hayley caught her eye and shook her head. She wanted Eve's unfiltered reaction.

"As I said, I wanted to find out who Micah's father is. I wanted to leave Micah with him while I tried to clear my name. I came to Royal, rented a room and headed over here, to this hospital, thinking that I'd ask about DNA and how paternity tests worked. I was crossing the parking lot, holding Micah's baby carrier, when I felt incredibly dizzy. I thought I was about to pass out so I put the carrier on the closest car. I think it was a Mercedes, I'm not sure. I made it to the hospital entrance. Before I could tell anyone about leaving Micah, I blacked out."

"Do you know what caused you to lose consciousness?" Hayley asked.

Eve looked at Sierra. "Off the record?"

"Absolutely," Sierra responded.

Eve placed a hand over her heart. "Like my sister, I have a heart condition. I saw the doctor earlier and my heart problems will keep me in the hospital for a few weeks." Tears rolled down her lovely face. "I can't look after Micah and I don't want him going into the system."

Hayley didn't either so she pulled up Cammie's number on her cell phone and dialed, and a few minutes later she had Cammie's assurance that she and Drake were happy to keep Micah with them for the foreseeable future and that they would even bring Micah to see Eve in a day or two.

"I'll give you Cammie's number. She said you are welcome to call at any time," Hayley told Eve.

Eve wiped her tears away and managed a tremulous smile. "Thank you. Are you going to arrest me?"

Hayley shook her head. "Not today. As I said, there's no arrest warrant out but don't do a runner, okay?"

"If I do, I might pass out again," Eve told her and followed up her sleepy statement with a huge yawn.

Hayley used her index finger to tell Sierra that they needed to wrap it up and Sierra nodded. "I'm writing a story about the history of the TCC club, so can I dig into the story about the kid left on a doorstep a century ago?" Sierra asked.

Eve nodded. "Knock yourself out. Feel free to try and discover who Micah's father is, too, if you like."

Sierra nodded enthusiastically. "I like."

Hayley bid Eve goodbye and they walked to the door and slipped out of her room. Outside, they walked down the hallway toward the elevator banks, both of them deep in thought.

"Well, that was interesting," Hayley said.

"Very," Sierra said. "We need to discuss it a lot more. What about tomorrow afternoon while we get our hair and makeup done at the Saint Tropez Salon?"

Hayley sent her a "get real" look. "I don't have an appointment at the salon and, even if I did, I can't afford their prices. I'm on a cop's salary, remember?"

"A call came in on your answering machine when I was at your house reading Arielle's diary. Your mother booked the appointment and has paid for it. I called them and they are squeezing me in at the same time."

"Have fun on your own," Hayley told Sierra. She saw the small frown of disapproval on Sierra's face and shrugged. "Look, my mother is flying to Europe tomorrow and will never know if I make the appointment or not."

Sierra grinned. "Nope. According to her message, she's persuaded your father to delay their departure and intends to check on whether you are there or not. If not, she, and your dad, will fly to Royal and personally escort you to the salon."

Hayley tipped her head up to the ceiling and released a vicious curse.

"Don't you check your messages?" Sierra asked,
curious.

"No," Hayley retorted, walking into the empty elevator. "And now you know why."

Five

It was official—he'd walked into the TCC ballroom with the most beautiful woman in the room.

Hayley was, possibly, the most gorgeous woman he'd ever encountered.

Standing by the bar, Jackson watched Hayley greet Cammie and Drake, her silver gown sparkling in the romantic lighting of the ballroom. The body-skimming dress highlighted her subtle curves, dipping deeply to show hints of her fabulous breasts. Breasts that didn't need any support. Her lack of a bra had Jackson wondering if she wore any underwear at all.

Eyes up, dude. Stop looking at her breasts, stop waiting for a peek of a luscious, bare long leg to appear between the thigh-high slit of her dress. The strappy sandals on her feet took her height to over six feet and her deep, dark lustrous hair was curled and parted to one side and swept over one bare shoulder.

Hayley in her cop uniform and wearing minimal makeup was lovely but this Hayley, with smoky eyes and bold red lipstick, was knee-dissolving, dick-hardening, breath-stealing sensational.

He couldn't take his eyes off her.

Not that he wanted to...

Thanking the bartender for his whiskey, he picked up a glass of champagne for Hayley and walked across the crowded room to join her, Cammie and Drake. Hayley took her glass and thanked him.

"Who's looking after the baby, Cam?" Jackson asked.

"Ainsley," Cammie replied. She looked at Hayley. "She's Drake's stepsister. By the way, I love your dress, Hayley. You look sensational."

Hayley pulled a face. "I'd feel far more comfortable in my uniform."

Jackson didn't doubt that for a second. Hayley might look stunning but now and again she tugged at the neckline of her dress or fiddled with her hair. She far preferred to be complimented on her brains and her competency than on her looks, and Jackson, used to women who put a lot of stock in their appearance, found her attitude refreshing.

Jackson forced his eyes to move off Hayley and looked at his old friend, immediately noticing her tight lips and the worry flashing in her eyes. He sent Cammie a reassuring smile. "I'm sure Rafe will be here soon."

It was a lie. He had no idea whether Rafe was coming or not.

Cammie bit the inside of her lip. "I hope so, Jackson. Wouldn't it be awesome if we could all spend Thanksgiving dinner together?"

Right, Thanksgiving was in a few weeks. Not having a family, he usually joined the Wentworths for Thanksgiving dinner and spent the rest of the holiday weekend working.

If Rafael didn't come to this ball, then he'd head to Miami and kick his ass, Jackson decided, coming back to the subject they were discussing. Cammie had been devastated when Rafael left Royal, and his half-sister had nothing to do with Rafe's feud with his father. All she wanted was to get to know her big brother.

His eyes met Drake's and at that moment Jackson knew that Cam's fiancé would gladly accompany him to Miami to kick Rafe's ass if he disappointed his sister. It was nice to know that Drake had Cam's best interests at heart. Love and loyalty weren't always, as he knew from watching his mother, a given in marriage.

"Tobias is going to be making the big announcement soon. I hope he's here for that," Cammie fretted.

"Don't get your hopes up, darling," Drake cautioned her.

Jackson heard a buzz of excitement and, using his height, he looked across the tops of many heads to the entrance and his eyebrows lifted.

Well, well, well, the prodigal son had returned. No kicking would be needed.

"Cammie, he's here," Jackson quietly told her.

A huge smile split her face and she put her hand on her heart. "Oh, that's amazing. Where is he? I can't wait to see him."

Jackson looked across the room to watch Rafael and sighed. Rafael was wearing his poker face but Jackson immediately noticed his tight lips and tense shoulders and knew that his old friend was already regretting his decision to return to Royal.

"Don't rush him, baby. Let him come to you," Drake suggested.

Jackson nodded. "That's good advice, Cam."

"Officer Lopez."

Hayley whipped around and teetered on her heels and Jackson caught her elbow to steady her. He shook hands with Nate Battle, Royal's sheriff, and greeted Amanda, his always lovely wife.

Nate turned to Hayley and lifted both eyebrows. "Who are you and what have you done with my boot-wearing, ass-kicking officer?"

Hayley narrowed her eyes at him. "Hey, I'm dressed up like this because you wouldn't let me wear my uniform." Hayley winced at her frank reply and hastily tacked on a "sir."

"I should've. That dress is…" Nate waved his hands, looking like a distressed father about to order his teenage daughter to wear a much longer skirt.

"You look lovely, Hayley," Amanda jumped in, nailing her husband with a "shut it" look. "And who wants to be photographed wearing that ugly uniform?"

"Me!" Hayley and Nate Battle said in unison and their companions laughed at their mutual distress.

Amanda rolled her eyes. "Well, do try and smile when you accept your awards. No hard-eyed cop grimaces, please."

"I don't see why we even have to do this," Hayley grumbled. "None of us want recognition. It's not necessary!"

"The town is deeply appreciative of Nate's work during the tornado that ripped through here in 2013 and for your and your fellow officers' service during the COVID-19 pandemic," Cammie quietly stated.

Nate tugged at the collar of his white dress shirt. "That's what we do, what we signed up for. We don't need thanks."

"Well, thanks is what you're going to get so suck it up, cupcake," Amanda briskly told him before looking at Hayley. "You, too, buttercup."

Hayley narrowed her eyes at Amanda, who laughed. "Oh, relax, Hayley! I've known you for far too long to be intimidated by your 'I've shot people for less' look." She patted Hayley on the arm. "Besides, you're not armed so I'm safe."

Amanda tugged Nate away to join another group across the room, and Jackson watched Hayley as she tracked their departure. Nate took two steps before retracing his steps back to Hayley.

"I meant to tell you that I took a call from a captain in the Miami PD earlier today," Nate quietly told her.

Despite her fancy dress and Hollywood hair, Hayley immediately morphed into cop mode, her lips flattening and her eyes narrowing. "And?"

"She's in the clear and they no longer consider her a suspect."

Nate's words were vague enough to sound ambiguous but Jackson knew enough from Hayley to assume they were talking about Eve Martin, suspected of embezzlement in Miami.

Hayley nodded. "Good to know. Thanks, boss."

Nate darted a look at his wife, saw that her attention was elsewhere and raised his eyebrows. "Tailored jacket, Glock under my arm. You?"

Before Hayley could reply, Amanda called her husband and Nate left without waiting for an answer to his question.

But Jackson needed to know...

He looked at her tiny clutch bag, thinking that there was no way she could've stuffed a weapon into a bag just big enough to carry her phone. And her dress was painted on her, falling into silver waves from her hips down.

No way was she wearing her weapon.

But the thought of her carrying made him hot. Seriously hot. Like take-her-out-of-the-room-and-run-his-hands-over-her-body hot.

Jackson placed his hand on the bare skin of her lower back and dropped his head to talk into her ear. "He was joking, right?"

Hayley looked up at him through extralong eyelashes. "Nope, I'm a cop and I always carry."

Jackson closed his eyes and shook his head. Man, she was something else. A curious combination of savage and sexy and stunning.

"I don't believe you," he said because, really, no way was she wearing a skimpy designer gown and carrying a concealed weapon.

Hayley sent him a low, slow, wanna-bet smile. "I have a Ruger LCP, very small and lightweight, strapped to my left leg. Unless I decide to do the cancan, nobody will know it's there."

Thank God. And all his angels and archangels. Then Hayley placed a hand on his lapel and her breath caressed the shell of his ear. "I'd offer to show it to you but…"

"But?" Jackson's one-word question came out as a strangled gasp.

Her bare, golden shoulders lifted in a casual shrug. "But someone very stupid said I'm too young for you so…"

"What an idiot," Jackson said, his fingers digging into her hip.

Hayley's red lips curved upward. "I thought so." She lifted her chin and gestured to the French doors leading onto a balcony. "Want to come to look at the stars with me?"

If she was old enough to wear a slip-looking dress and carry a weapon, he wasn't going to joke around with her. "If we go outside, my hands are going to be all over your body."

Hayley looked at him with those dark, dark eyes. "Screw the stars," she stated and walked toward the balcony.

Jackson, feeling a little disconcerted and very turned on, followed her.

* * *

Hayley stepped onto the empty-of-people balcony, walked down its length to where it was dark and shivered. Her thin dress was no barrier to the cold and her nipples instantly pebbled and goose bumps broke over her skin. But being a little cold was a price she was very prepared to pay if it meant being in Jackson's arms, having his mouth on hers.

Hayley heard the door close behind her and slowly turned, her breath catching at the sight of a tuxedo-clad Jackson slowly making his way to where she stood.

There was something about a man in a tux...

No, there was something about Jackson. Underneath his urbane, charming facade, Hayley sensed something untamed and a little feral and she wanted to taste that wildness on her tongue. She was tired of dancing around her attraction to him. She wanted him and, judging by the possessive look in his eyes, he wanted her.

This was chemistry, pheromones, desire...two healthy people who wanted nothing more than to know each other in the most biblical of ways.

She was still Hayley, she told herself, still independent and forthright, still her own person, and nothing she did with, or to, Jackson would change that.

Hayley felt a flicker of trepidation when the back of Jackson's knuckles drifted over her cheekbone, down her jaw. So sweet, so tender.

Hard and fast she could handle; sweet and tender scared her.

She was physically attracted to Jackson but she intended to remain emotionally detached. She had things to do, goals to reach. She didn't have the time or the inclination to dive into a relationship…

"A million thoughts are buzzing around your over-active brain, Hayley Lopez," Jackson said, placing his hands on her waist and nuzzling his mouth against her ear. "Why don't you stop trying to control the world for ten seconds?"

Hayley placed her hands against the lapels of his jacket, resisting the urge to sink into his body and his heat. "I'm not trying to control the world."

"No, you're just trying to control your reaction to me," Jackson murmured. His hand moved to her bare back and dipped down between her dress and her bare skin. "Don't. Be honest with me. Do you want me?"

She couldn't lie, not about this. "Yes."

"Do you want to want me?"

"No."

Jackson chuckled as he raked his lips up the side of her throat, before pulling her earlobe between his teeth. How could such a small area of her skin be so sensitive? How was it possible that she had a highway of lust running from her earlobe to between her legs?

Jackson's bare fingers drifted over the top of her bare butt and stopped when he found the very thin, almost invisible cord to her thong. "I was wondering whether you were wearing any underwear."

"Only panties," Hayley told him. Was she sounding breathless? That was new.

Jackson pulled back to look at her and his hot gaze on her breasts caused her nipples to harden. Hayley watched, mesmerized, as his eyes darkened and he lifted his hand to run the tip of his index finger over her nipple. Hayley shuddered. He was only touching her with his finger yet every nerve ending on her body felt alive, like she was plugged into a universal source of energy.

"You are so incredibly beautiful, Hayley."

No, she wasn't, but right now, with his eyes on her, she felt like she was. Beautiful, strong, feminine, powerful...

Hayley lifted her hand to curl it around his neck. "Is that all you are going to do, Jackson? Touch me there?"

A small smile lifted the corners of Jackson's mouth. "You don't like it?"

"Oh, I like it. I was just wondering if there's more to come."

Jackson moved his finger to her other breast, rubbing the palm of his hand over her nipple and causing Hayley to whimper. "I want you, more than anything in the world. I want to take your mouth, kiss you senseless and dig my fingers into your hair. I want to skim my hands up your truly excellent legs and slide my fingers inside you and make you shudder in my arms."

Hayley felt her womb pulsate, her skin prickle. Oh, God, she couldn't wait. She wanted all of that, all of him. She wanted him on her, sliding his long length into her, filling her and completing her. And she wanted all of that...right damn now.

"What are you waiting for?" Hayley asked, her voice husky with need. Needing to show him that she was very on board with anything he wanted to do to her, she placed her palm on his long, rock-hard erection, curling her fingers as best she could around him. Jackson sucked in a harsh breath before releasing a low groan, pushing himself into her palm.

"In case you didn't get the message, this is me giving you the green light."

"Ah, honey…" Jackson dropped his face into her neck.

"Kiss me, Jackson."

Jackson lifted his head to look at her, deep blue eyes frustrated. "I'd love to but if I start, I won't stop and they are about to announce the honorees. I don't want to mess your hair and makeup and if I start kissing and touching you, I know I will."

"I can't tell you how little I care," Hayley muttered. She didn't care about the award but she did care about knowing what it felt like to be on the receiving end of Jackson's bedroom-based skills.

"God, you smell amazing," Jackson said. "You always do."

He pulled back and lifted one hand to her face, his thumb lightly stroking her cheekbone. "When the gala is done, when you have seen and spoken to everyone, received your award and done your thing, let me know and I'll be more than glad to divest you of that dress and your weapon. Though we might keep those sexy shoes and the thong on. I'm going to make you scream, Lopez."

Hayley stared at him, her heart thundering in her chest. "You promise?"

"Yeah. You give me the word and we're out of here."

Hayley picked up his wrist, pushed back his shirt and jacket to look at his slim, elegant watch. Piaget? Good taste, Michaels. "It's eight thirty. We're out of here by eleven thirty, awards or no awards."

Jackson grinned. "God, you are the bossiest woman I've ever met."

Hayley's grin flashed, lighting up her dark eyes. "But you like it."

Jackson started at her for twenty seconds before he nodded. "Yeah, I do," he admitted. "But I have no damn idea why."

"It's because I keep you on your toes," Hayley told him, threading her fingers through his. She tugged him toward the doors. "Let's go back in and I'll find whoever is running this show and tell them to move it along."

Jackson's laughter rumbled over her. "Are you that desperate to get your hands on me, Lopez?"

Hayley spun on her heels to look him dead in the eye. "Yes, the sooner we sleep together, the sooner we can work each other out of our systems and get back to normal. Do you disagree or have a problem with that?"

"No. God, *no*."

Damn straight. She didn't, either.

Hayley thought that sleeping together would allow them to move on, but Jackson suspected it would just complicate the situation further.

Oh, he wasn't going to back out of their deal—he wasn't a fool or a saint—but he knew that there was a good chance that instead of being able to walk away with a brisk, it-was-fun goodbye, they'd find ways to justify their decision to keep sleeping together. Somehow, Jackson knew he would not be satisfied with a one-night stand, or even a one-week stand. Hayley provided too many challenges, excited him on a deeper fundamental level. She had depths to plumb, secrets to discover, and all of that took time.

And when he was done on his quest to explore Hayley-land, where would that leave him? Would he find himself even more entranced with her than he currently was, craving her with every beat of his heart instead of with every third beat? Would he catch feelings? Would she?

Jackson headed to the bar, rubbing his neck as he avoided various people wanting to speak to him. He ordered a drink from the bartender, took the shot and threw it down, gesturing for the bartender to pour him another. Deciding that he needed some air, he headed back toward the balcony, hoping that no one would follow him out.

He needed a few minutes alone, to think and regroup.

If something developed between him and Hayley, where would it go? Could it go anywhere as they were at vastly different places in their lives, in their careers? He was established, successful, while she was still trying to make her mark. She was feisty and challenging but she still had a streak of idealism found only in the still young, the ones who believed that they could make a difference. And Hayley probably could, if love and marriage and a relationship didn't get in the way.

Jackson leaned his hip against the railing and stared into the dark Texas night. Usually, he didn't give his relationships—okay, hookups—this much thought but he was coming to accept that Hayley was a bright comet in a sky filled with pinprick stars. And because she was different, he had to change his thought patterns and consider all his options.

And that meant admitting that Hayley—too young, too independent, too in his face—could be the one woman who could change his mind about remaining a bachelor. She was the only woman he could imagine having in his life on a long-term basis.

But their age difference could and would cause problems. When he was twenty, she was seven, for God's sake. She was building her knowledge base, still finding her feet in a career, and he could retire tomorrow without a second thought.

He was strong-willed and was used to calling the shots. She would never stand for him being who he was, a confident alpha guy who liked being right. They'd fight. They'd yell.

They were equally bossy and because he was older and had more life experience, he'd expect to be the one leading, Hayley a step behind.

He'd grown up in a house with two dominant personalities vying for control and he didn't want to put himself in that situation. Neither did he want to raise kids—God, he was thinking about kids!—in a war zone. Hayley wasn't a shrinking violet. Nobody who walked away from her rich, generous family to carve her path could be. But Jackson didn't think he could

be with someone who would question his every decision, who was headstrong and willful.

His mother had emotionally shattered his father in
her quest to show him that she was physically, mentally and emotionally tougher than him.

If he and Hayley started seeing each other, Jackson
knew that they were walking into a field filled with
quicksand and vents emitting sulfuric acid. Eventually,
they'd start to dissolve...

So maybe it would be better not to get involved. Not
to sleep together.

But that wasn't going to happen. He needed her and
he intended to have her.

And this, Jackson realized, was how his father
stepped onto the path of self-destruction...

"Evening, Jack."

A deep voice pulled him from his thoughts and
Jackson lifted his head to see his friend Gabriel Carrington standing a few feet from him, a glass of whiskey in his hand. Jackson shook his hand and echoed his
stance, leaning back against the balcony and crossing
one ankle over the other.

"It's been a while," Gabe said, lifting his glass in
a silent toast.

"I haven't been as active in the TCC lately as I
should've been," Jackson admitted.

"Yeah, I heard you are trying to develop the land
around Stone Lake."

Jackson heard a discordant note in Gabe's voice and
frowned. "You don't approve?"

"Not up to me to approve or disapprove. But I do

know that Bubba is not going to sell. Not now and not ever. He's a stubborn old coot and he's attached to his land.

"He lost both his sons, one in a car accident when he was a teenager and the other died in Iraq. They, and his wife, are all buried on that land, as are his daddy, momma and both sets of grandparents. The land has been in his family for four generations and he's determined to die there," Gabriel explained. He looked through the French doors and nodded in Hayley's direction. "Did Hayley not tell you?"

"I didn't ask," Jackson admitted, embarrassed. "But, to be honest, we're either fighting or fighting our attraction so we haven't had many conversations, either."

A brief smile hit Gabe's eyes. "She'll keep things interesting, that's for sure." Gabriel took a long swallow of his drink and nodded to the crowded room beyond the French doors. "I wonder what my male ancestors would think of the TCC today. So many members, African Americans and Latinos. Women members, too!" Gabriel mock-grabbed his heart. "Shock! Horror!"

Jackson recalled that Gabriel's great-great-grandfather was one of the earliest members of the TCC. "It's good progress, though."

"I agree. And my grandfathers can keep spinning in their graves."

Jackson turned his back on the ballroom and leaned his forearms on the railing off the balcony. He'd been hearing rumors about Gabe for a while and had been meaning to invite him out for a beer, wanting to give him a heads-up about what was being said about him

Get up to 4
FREE FABULOUS BOOKS
You Love!

To thank you for being a loyal reader we'd like to send you up to 4 FREE BOOKS, absolutely free.

Just write "YES" on the Loyal Reader Voucher and we'll send you up to 4 Free Books and Free Mystery Gifts, altogether worth over $20, as a way of saying thank you for being a loyal reader.

Try **Harlequin® Desire** books featuring the worlds of the American elite with juicy plot twists, delicious sensuality and intriguing scandal.

Try **Harlequin Presents®** Larger-print books featuring the glamourous lives of royals and billionaires in a world of exotic locations, where passion knows no bounds.

Or **TRY BOTH!**

We are so glad you love the books as much as we do and can't wait to send you great new books.

So don't miss out, return your Loyal Reader Voucher Today!

Pam Powers

LOYAL READER
FREE BOOKS VOUCHER

YES! I Love Reading, please send me up to 4 FREE BOOKS and Free Mystery Gifts from the series I select.

Just write in "YES" on the dotted line below then return this card today and we'll send your free books & gifts asap!

➡ YES ⬅

Which do you prefer?

☐ **Harlequin Desire®**
225/326 HDL GRGA

☐ **Harlequin Presents® Larger Print**
176/376 HDL GRGA

☐ **BOTH**
225/326 & 176/376
HDL GRGM

FIRST NAME	LAST NAME

ADDRESS

APT.#	CITY

STATE/PROV.	ZIP/POSTAL CODE

EMAIL ☐ Please check this box if you would like to receive newsletters and promotional emails from Harlequin Enterprises ULC and its affiliates. You can unsubscribe anytime.

HD/HP-520-LR21

in town. Gabe could choose to either quash the rumors or ignore them but at least he would know what was being said about him.

"The rumor mill is saying that you are looking for the perfect wife and that you have hired a high-profile international matchmaker," Jackson said, keeping his tone flat.

Jackson expected Gabe to immediately refute his words but he took a while to respond. He was about to reply when Brett opened one French door and told them to get inside, that the formalities were starting.

They moved toward the door and Jackson waited for Gabriel to confirm or deny the gossip. His patience exhausted, Jackson bumped his shoulder and frowned at him. "Well? What's going on?"

Gabriel sent him an enigmatic smile. "Have a good night. Let's get together soon. And good luck with the lady-cop. She's a firecracker."

Yeah, he was going to need it.

Hayley was both touched and appreciative of Tobias Wentworth's pledge to pay for the college education of all children of the Royal hospital workers and first responders, which included the members of Royal PD. She was a child of extreme wealth, and her father had already made provisions to pay for all his grandchildren's education, but Hayley appreciated the gesture. Her relationship with her parents was a minor war zone with both parties jostling for position but she knew she was still loved.

She frustrated her family and they frustrated her

more but she was still a part of the Lopez clan. Two of her brothers were in attendance tonight and, apart from a quick "hi" and a hug, she'd, so far, managed to avoid a long conversation with them.

But she'd felt their eyes on her, seen their frowns when they realized Jackson was her date. Luis and Miguel occasionally cut her some slack so there was a fifty-fifty chance of them reporting back to their parents. She could only hope this was one of those times or else she'd be bombarded with questions from her mother first thing tomorrow morning.

Hayley, standing next to Sierra, looked across the room to see Jackson talking to some men at the bar and she sighed, wishing it was time to leave. She was sick of making small talk, her face was sore from smiling, and if one more person complimented her for doing her damn job, she might just whip out her gun and shoot herself, or them.

She wasn't a spotlight-y type of person. She just wanted to do her job. And nail Jackson.

Sierra jammed her elbow into her ribs. "Stop sighing, for God's sake!"

Hayley moved her plaque from one hand to the other, wishing she could toss it under the table and forget about it. "What time is it?"

Sierra looked at her bracelet watch. "A little after ten."

God, ninety minutes of torture left. *Ack.*

Hayley looked across at Jackson, saw him looking at her, and her entire body prickled under the heat of his gaze. His eyes moved down her neck, across her collarbone, across her breasts and slowly, oh, so slowly, drifted over her stomach and her lower body. Every inch of her skin heated and prickled and when his eyes stopped somewhere around her calves, he lifted one eyebrow.

Thong and shoes are staying on.

Hayley nodded in response to his silent order and Jackson's eyes heated with passion. Yeah, he wasn't as unaffected as he was pretending to be.

Sierra waved a hand in front of her face. "Can you two dial it down, please? You both just shot up the temperature in the room by a hundred degrees."

Hayley widened her eyes to look innocent. "I have no idea what you are talking about."

"Please," Sierra scoffed. "You are so getting lucky tonight."

Hayley laughed, unable to pretend. She placed a hand on her chest. "God, I hope so."

"Lucky bitch," Sierra said, without a trace of rancor in her voice.

"Who is the tall guy standing by the French doors?" Sierra asked, moving to stand between her and her view of Jackson. It was a good call on Sierra's part since she couldn't stop looking his way.

Hayley looked across the room to see Rafael Wentworth lifting a glass to his stern mouth, looking like he'd rather be facing a firing squad than hobnobbing with the great and good of Royal.

Hayley sympathized. "That's Cammie's half brother Rafael."

"Good-looking guy," Sierra said. Biracial, Mexican and Caucasian, he was tall and broad and broody. "Where is he based?"

"Miami," Hayley replied.

"Eve is from Miami, and so was Arielle," Sierra stated.

"The thought has crossed my mind more than a few times this evening," Hayley replied. "But it's a big city. The chances of them knowing each other are slim."

"She did write his name in caps letters on a black page in her diary," Sierra pointed out.

She knew that. "It's a long shot, Sierra."

"It's the only shot we have," Sierra insisted as they both watched Rafael drain his glass. A hovering waiter took his glass, spoke, and when Rafael shook his head, Hayley assumed he was refusing another drink. Did that mean he was leaving? And if he left and went straight back to Miami, she might not have another chance to speak with him, to read his body language, to look for cracks in his composure.

It wasn't the right time or place but it might be the only chance she had.

"Go talk to him, Hayley!" Sierra urged her.

Hayley looked around for Sheriff Battle, didn't see him and winced. This was a social occasion and Rafael wouldn't appreciate being ambushed, but what other choice did she have? Her window of opportunity was narrowing…

Shit. Hayley pushed her glass of champagne and award into Sierra's hands, picked up the hem of her dress and pushed through the crowd toward Rafael.

When she saw that he was heading for the exit, she changed direction to cut him off before he got there.

Stepping out from between two groups of people, including some members of the Royal Reporters—i.e., Royal's most skilled gossips—Hayley pulled a smile up onto her face.

"Mr. Wentworth? May I have a word?"

Rafael stopped and frowned at her. "Who are you?"

"Officer Hayley Lopez, Royal PD," she automatically replied. She cursed herself for her instinctive reply. She'd all but announced to everyone surrounding them that she wanted to talk to Rafael in an official capacity.

"Can we chat, in private?" Hayley asked, forcing a smile onto her face.

The cold expression on Rafael's expression didn't change. "I think here is just fine."

Every ear in a six-foot radius was flapping. This was so not a good idea. Hayley shook her head. "Maybe we can catch up in the morning."

"I might not be available tomorrow so it's now or never—" Rafael's eyes skimmed her body to come back to her face "—*Officer.*"

Double, triple shit.

Right, she was going to have to be super subtle. Putting her back to their audience, she lowered her voice. "You live in Miami, right?"

Rafael lifted a shoulder in a casual shrug. "Mostly."

"I was wondering if you ever met two women in Miami, one Eve Martin or her sister, Arielle."

Rafael folded his arms across his chest and tipped his head to the side. "Why?"

Hayley knew that a few people had shuffled closer and all the conversation in the immediate vicinity had stopped, the gala guests dropping all pretense that they weren't eavesdropping. Thanks to Royal's superhot gossip line, she did not doubt that everyone in Royal knew that she, and Sierra, were trying to track down baby Micah's father.

"There's a mention of your name in Arielle Martin's diary."

"And that means what?"

"Can we talk somewhere private, Mr. Wentworth?" Hayley asked, on the point of begging.

"No point because I don't know anyone with those names." Rafael's smile didn't reach his eyes. "If that is all?"

If she was in her uniform, hell, if they were anywhere else, she'd pull out her phone and show him a picture of Eve. But she was at a very upmarket gala, wearing next to nothing, and if she pushed harder, she'd cause a scene.

And then her boss would ream her a new one and she'd be riding a desk for the foreseeable future. Hayley nodded. "Thank you for your time, Mr. Wentworth."

Hayley stepped away, straightened her shoulders and took a glass of champagne from a hovering waiter holding a tray. Her duty was done. Now she could have some fun.

Turning to an elderly man wearing an exquisite tuxedo and a black Stetson, she asked him for the time.

"It's ten twenty."

Crap, still an hour and a bit before they could leave.

Dammit, who knew time could move so slowly?

Six

Fifteen minutes until they could leave and Jackson could not wait. In twenty-five minutes, thanks to his stupidly fast Chiron, Hayley Lopez would be naked and he'd finally, finally know whether reality could compete with his imagination.

Knowing that he would be in control of one of the world's fastest cars, he'd opted to limit his alcohol consumption so when a bartender turned to take his order, he asked for a club soda.

Jackson took his drink, turned and noticed Rafael behind him. He smiled, genuinely pleased to see his oldest friend. "Rafe, it's good to see you. I'm glad you could make it."

Rafael didn't return his greeting and the handshake they exchanged was ultra-brief. Jackson frowned.

Okay, he hadn't expected a manly hug but neither did he expect such a cold shoulder.

"Everything okay?" Jackson asked, keeping his voice low.

Rafael walked to the end of the bar and Jackson followed. Dammit, he hoped that Rafe and Tobias hadn't exchanged words on the first night Rafael was back in town, but anything was possible when it came to them. They were more alike than either cared to admit. If they had exchanged words, he hoped Cammie didn't hear them as her heart was set on a Thanksgiving family reunion.

"Everything okay, bud?" Jackson quietly asked when they had a modicum of privacy.

"Oh, peachy," Rafael retorted after ordering a double bourbon from the bartender. "After an awkward handshake with my father, witnessed by everyone in the room, I remembered why I hated being here. And everyone keeps telling me how wonderful my father is. And what's with his transformation into Mr. Nice Guy?"

"Danae's death did that, Rafe."

Rafael waved his words away. "And they keep asking me whether we've kissed and made up and whether I am staying in Royal."

"Are you?"

Rafael took a large sip of his drink. "I'd rather shove a branding fork against my cheek," Rafael shot back. "I've got Cammie constantly hugging me and looking at me like I hang the moon—"

"Drake does that for her now," Jackson quipped, hoping to break the tension with a joke.

Rafael did not look amused.

Okay, something else must've happened to throw Rafe off his stride. "What's going on, Rafael?"

"Well, apart from being the black sheep and everyone watching me to see whether I'm going to argue with my father, I had some woman publicly demanding to know whether I met two women in Miami, sisters with the surname of Martin."

"Who asked you that?" But Jackson suspected he knew.

"Young, gorgeous, wearing a silver dress. She said she's with the Royal PD."

Jackson silently dropped a series of F-bombs. Dammit, Hayley. What the hell was she doing questioning Rafael Wentworth, one of Miami's richest men, at one of the most prestigious events in Texas? Apart from the fact that there was a time and place for everything, she was off duty.

"Then, in the men's room, some dude nudges me and asks me if I'm the father of the abandoned baby."

Oh, shit.

"So, I've been back in Royal approximately four hours and the rumors are already flying that I'm this baby's father. Goddammit, Jackson! Given the fact that I was all but abandoned by my father, I would never be so careless to get a woman pregnant and I would never, ever leave her to fend for herself!"

Jackson looked around the room and took in the

edgy, vibey atmosphere. It wasn't difficult to miss the covert glances, the whispers behind forced smiles.

And, with the blink of an eye, he was transported back to parties his parents hosted or attended. His mother had been a master of manipulation, able to turn a fun party sour by dropping a couple of vicious comments. She'd needed to be the center of attention and frequently achieved that by spreading unsubstantiated rumors (some about his dad) and by spouting off-the-wall and offensive political and religious conspiracy theories just to irritate the guests and to get a reaction.

Like his mother, Hayley blundered into situations without thought to the consequences.

And, like his mother, she was strong, independent and forthright. *Uncontrollable.*

He should be running as hard and as fast as he could in the opposite direction. He'd watched this movie, and it always ended with blood being shed.

"I'll do what I can to quash the rumors but you know this town, the truth has never got in the way of a juicy bit of gossip," Jackson told Rafael.

Rafael raked his hand through his hair. "I shouldn't have come back tonight."

"I'm glad you did. And so are Tobias and Cammie," Jackson told him, briefly gripping his shoulder.

"I'm going to go," Rafael told him, and grimaced when he saw the still-crowded room.

"There's a door behind me. If you use it, it'll take you into a staff corridor. Turn left, left again and you'll hit the parking lot," Jackson suggested.

Rafael nodded. "I'd ask you to share a bottle with me but I'm in a foul mood."

So, suddenly, was he. "Thanks, but I have a fight to pick with a goddess carrying a gun."

Rafael's eyes widened and he lifted his hands. "I'm not even going to ask."

Over Rafael's shoulder, Jackson saw Hayley walking over to him, a small smile on her luscious lips. Out of the corner of his eye, he watched Rafael slip away and when Hayley stopped next to him, she placed a hand on his forearm and lifted to talk in his ear. "Ready to go?"

Yes. No. He didn't know.

He should be bolting, not wanting to kiss her senseless. She was trouble.

Everything-is-bigger-in-Texas trouble.

Not wanting an audience for whatever came next, Jackson gripped her elbow and led her through the door Rafael used a minute before. When they stepped into the narrow hallway, Rafe was gone.

"Was it necessary to ask Rafael whether he is baby Micah's father?"

Confusion flashed across her face. "What?"

"Everyone in there thinks that Rafe is Arielle's lover and that he abandoned her." He heard the harsh accusation in his tone and knew that he was using her questioning of Rafe to create some distance between them. Distance he desperately needed.

"But why?" Hayley asked. "All I did was ask him whether he knew the Martin sisters."

"You accosted him in front of a bunch of people..." Jackson trailed off, remembering that he'd seen Grant

Webber in the group standing close to Rafael earlier. Grant hated Tobias with a passion bordering on pathological. And if he was in earshot of Hayley and Rafe's conversation, he could easily imagine him spreading a vicious, untrue rumor just to mess with Tobias.

"I did not accost him!" Hayley retorted, hands on her hips. "I asked him, very politely, whether he knew them.

"Before I mentioned the sisters, I asked whether we could meet in the morning, and he said he might not be here," Hayley added.

"Still, it could've waited!" he insisted, digging in his heels. Yeah, he could be stubborn, too. Why couldn't she be easygoing, lovely but uninteresting, unexciting? How could she, so young and so vital, tie him up in inescapable knots?

"In your opinion," Hayley whipped back.

"You caused a scene and you spoiled the Wentworths' evening!" Jackson stated, knowing that he was trying to pick a fight and not much caring.

"Wow, I did all of that with a two-minute conversation? I'm better than I thought," Hayley replied, her sarcasm levels sky-high.

"I was doing my job!"

Jackson scrubbed his hands over his face. "There's a time and a place for everything, Hayley, and tonight wasn't it. Rafael didn't want to be here in the first place and you harassing him has his temper fired up. If he leaves again, I'm going to blame you."

"That's not fair!"

No, it wasn't. But neither was it fair that he wanted

to shake her as much as he wanted to kiss her, that he was as irritated as he was turned on. Women didn't get to him like this. He always managed to keep his emotions under control, preferring cold, hard logic to fights in corridors.

"The room is filled with some of the wealthiest, most influential people in the state, Hayley!"

"So?" Hayley asked, belligerently.

"So think before you speak!"

Hayley cocked her head to the side. "Are you done with the lecture?"

Yeah, he was done.

"I asked him a question, I didn't spread the rumor," Hayley told him, picking up the fabric of her dress to keep it off the grubby linoleum floor. "So you can take your judgmental attitude and shove it, Michaels.

"I don't care about wealth and status. I'm a cop, I do my job and sometimes that means inconveniencing people. Well, *tough*. I will always get to the truth, no matter how many toes, yours and your precious friend's included, I need to step on to get to the truth.

"I get enough lectures from my family and you are not my boss, so don't you ever lecture me again." Hayley grabbed the handle and pulled open the door. "And since you don't respect me and the way I do my job, you can go screw yourself."

Jackson winced.

"I'll find my own way home," Hayley said, back straight and her head held high. "I'd say thank you for a nice evening but it mostly wasn't."

* * *

At home, Hayley showered, scrubbed the makeup off her face and dragged her hair up into a messy up-knot. Wearing a tank top and loose pajama bottoms, she stomped into her kitchen and put the kettle on the gas stove. She needed to run, to pummel a punching bag, spar with her training partner, but since it was close to one in the morning, chamomile tea would have to do.

She doubted there was enough chamomile in the world to make her temper subside.

She hadn't done anything wrong! She'd asked Rafael Wentworth, a couple of times, whether they could talk privately, and when he refused to budge, she framed her questioning delicately. It wasn't like she demanded to know whether he was Arielle's lover using a bullhorn.

Okay, maybe asking him at the gala wasn't ideal but he *had* said that he might not be in Royal when the sun rose, so she hadn't much choice but to push him for answers.

It wasn't her fault that someone—and God help him or her if she found out who—started the rumor that he was baby Micah's father.

As for Jackson…

Hayley gripped the edge of the counter and stared down at her bare feet. He'd overreacted, and immediately chosen to believe the worst about her without hearing her out. He immediately aligned himself with the Wentworths, his loyalty to them unquestionable and absolute.

But his actions did tell her that when the chips were

down, that when she was backed into a corner, she couldn't rely on him for backup or for him to even consider her point of view. She was, as she always was, alone.

Her head pounding, Hayley dumped boiling water over a tea bag. Her family loved her but she didn't have their unqualified support. They loved her but would love, and like, her more if she came home, pursued a career within the Lopez group of companies, found a nice man to marry, had a couple of babies.

But Hayley had this strange and weird conviction that, as their daughter and sister, she should be loved no matter the path she chose to walk.

Love and acceptance should not be subject to whims and conditions.

Hayley picked up her cup and walked over to her sofa, curling up into the arm and tucking her feet under her butt. She knew she wasn't easy to love. Sometimes she thought she wasn't even easy to like. She was headstrong and opinionated, impulsive and determined and fully accepted that she wasn't everyone's cup of tea. Hell, she'd far preferred to be a handful of people's whiskey anyway.

But she was intensely disappointed that a two-minute conversation with Jackson's friend blew her plans for the evening out of the window. If she hadn't confronted Rafael about Arielle, she could be rolling around her bed right now, writhing under Jackson's hands, exploring his big, masculine body. If she had taken a moment to think, her evening would have ended with joy and not a joust.

But she couldn't get past the fact that all she'd done was ask a question...an innocuous one at that.

Asking a question shouldn't be a hanging offense; neither should it be a barrier to some bed-based fun.

Stupid man. And stupid her for sitting here, second-guessing herself and wishing she'd done something different...

Hayley heard a light knock on her door and she sat up and placed the cup on her coffee table, her head cocked. She heard another light rap and, without putting on a light, walked over to her door and looked through the peephole to see who was standing on her porch at 1:20 a.m.

Because Jackson was so tall, all she could see was the bottom part of his face, but she instantly recognized his sexy mouth and stubborn chin, the small scar on the corner of his bottom lip.

Hayley took off her chain, flipped her dead bolt and pulled open the door to her very late-night visitor. She wished she could say that he was unwelcome but, because she always tried to be honest with herself, he wasn't.

Hayley ignored the open collar of his shirt, his short stubble and his sensual scent, leaned her shoulder into the frame of the door and crossed her arms against her chest. "What do you want?"

Jackson's eyes flicked down her body, all the way to her toes, lingered on her tight nipples—it was cold, and she was wearing a skimpy top—and returned to her face.

"You."

Yeah, right. Hayley lifted her nose in the air. "You should've thought about that before you picked a fight with me earlier."

Jackson sent her a brooding look but didn't bite her baited hook. Damn, she was so tempted to just grab him by his jacket lapels and drag him into her hall.

And then she'd jump him…

Talk about being impulsive…

Hayley fought to keep her spine straight, to keep up the act of being a tough girl. But she was tired, and a little sad and a lot lonely. And horny, God, so horny. "Why are you here, Michaels?"

"I'm here because I always, always, keep my promises."

What was he talking about?

"I promised to make you scream and I want to keep that promise," Jackson calmly stated, his face impassive but his eyes a whirlpool of need and passion. "I'm pissed off, annoyed, beyond confused but I still want to take you to bed."

"Oh."

Oh? Was that the only word she could find? Apparently so since her brain just completely collapsed.

Hayley released an unhappy sigh. "How is it possible that I'm desperate to jump you? You're absolutely infuriating!"

A hint of amusement lightened Jackson's eyes. "I know that you hate it when I reference our age gap but experience has taught me that angry sex is a great way to release frustration and to deal with adrenaline. Anger can also work as an aphrodisiac. Science says that it gets your blood flowing and increases your heart rates and blood pressure."

"Thank you, Dr. Know-It-All," Hayley retorted.

Jackson stepped closer to her and curled his hand around her neck, dropping his forehead to rest against hers. "I'm annoyed with you and you're, obviously, still pissed at me but I swear on everything I believe in, that I'll make it good for you."

His honesty was refreshing and deeply appreciated. If he'd tried to BS her or sweet-talk her, then she would've kicked him to the curb.

"Yes or no, Hayley?"

Hayley was still in the process of nodding when Jackson wrapped his arms around her hips and hauled her up against him, his mouth instantly finding hers. Hayley framed his face with her hands, and poured herself into that kiss, trying to tell him that she needed more, that she needed every part of him, in her, around her.

Their tongues danced and dueled, fought and frolicked, and from somewhere far away, Hayley heard her front door slam shut. But all she cared about was that Jackson's erection was hard and wonderful and pushing into her stomach, that her nipples were rubbing against his chest, that her body was on fire and her heart felt like it was about to burst…

And she was okay with that.

Jackson pulled back to look at her, his eyes bright and intense. "You are so goddamn beautiful, Hayley. And you smell delicious. I can't wait to kiss you, taste you…"

But he'd already done that...*oh*. "Yes, please."

Jackson carried her into the lounge and laid her down on her sofa, the cushions sinking under their combined weight.

"This is my favorite fantasy coming true..." Jackson murmured.

Hayley lifted her mouth to capture his and their tongues clashed, fighting for control of the kiss. Bubbles of heat exploded in her belly, under her rib cage, in her soul, and her skin prickled with anticipation.

"Jackson." Hayley gasped his name, lifting her hips to push her mound into his steel-hard erection. "We have too many clothes on."

"Patience, spitfire."

Jackson pulled down her tank top with one finger, revealing her breasts, and he gently blew on her nipple and rubbed his stubble across the sensitive point. Hayley writhed beneath him and he finally, finally, took her into his mouth, alternatively lapping and sucking. This was pleasure, proper pleasure, Hayley decided as he switched to her other breast.

Her back arched and she released a series of disconnected words demanding more.

"Jackson, I need you." In case he was having trouble understanding her, Hayley decided to make her desires known. "I need you to put on a condom and come inside me."

Jackson released a little huff of laughter. "So bossy. But not in the bedroom, sweetheart. Here I control the pace. Be patient, Hayley-mine."

Jackson sat up and pulled her tank top over her head

and took a minute, and then another, to look at her. "Perfection, Hayley."

Hayley, unable to look away, ran her thumb over his jaw, down his thick neck. "I want to touch your amazing body."

"And you will…sometime." Jackson eased his fingers under the loose elastic of her pajamas and pushed the material down her hips.

"How am I supposed to take it slow when you look like this?" he asked.

"You're the one controlling the pace," Hayley pointed out a little crossly. "I'm ready for you and I need you."

"But you deserve more than a quick bang, sweetheart. Let me love you the way I want to. Please?"

How could she resist him? And why should she? Hayley dropped her hands to her sides and made her sigh overdramatic. "If you must."

Jackson's smile flashed on his face and in his eyes. "Oh, I must."

His hand trailed down her body and landed between her legs, and he unerringly found her happy spot. Hayley sucked in a harsh breath and clenched her legs against his fingers, wanting more but not sure she could bear it. His clever fingers explored her folds, sometimes just brushing her clit, sometimes rolling it in his fingers. Hayley pushed her head back into the cushion, her breathing harsh in the quiet air and broken only by her calling, *begging* his name. Jackson slid a finger inside her, then two and he lifted her higher, faster, encouraging her to fly.

This was pleasure that she'd never experienced before and it would be so easy to fly solo, to crash on her own, but she wanted Jackson with her, sharing this with her.

Jackson pulled back, quickly shed his clothes, and Hayley had a quick view of his ripped body—the man had muscles on his muscles—before he bent his head and placed his mouth on her, causing her to slam her eyes shut and release a series of joyful whimpers.

Hayley writhed on the cushions, her head whipping from side to side, and she knew she was close to an earth-shattering orgasm.

Putting both her hands on Jackson's shoulders, she pushed hard, forcing him to lift his head to look at her. His expression was feral, his eyes a deep, dangerous blue, his cheekbones flushed with desire.

"Are you asking me to stop?" Jackson demanded in a low growl.

As if she could. Hayley squeezed his shoulder. "No, God, please, don't. I'm so close but I want you to be inside me when I come. I want to come with you, on you."

Jackson knelt on the sofa, knees on either side of her, and reached down to grab his jacket. He pulled a strip of condoms from the inside pocket and ripped one off with his teeth, allowing the rest to fall to the floor. With a quick, practiced motion, he sheathed himself and, keeping his eyes on hers, positioned himself at her entrance.

Hayley waited a moment and when he didn't slide into her, waited some more. Placing her hands on his waist, she lifted her knees and wound her legs around his hips. Looking up, she lifted her eyebrows. "I might not be very experienced but even I know that this is more fun if you come on home, Michaels."

Jackson's soft laugh accompanied his quick, hard thrust. She expected a little pain, some discomfort—he was big and it had been a while—but all Hayley felt was a sense of rightness, of completion.

And pleasure. Mind-numbing, toe-curling, knee-dissolving pleasure.

Hayley released a moan but Jackson captured it in his mouth as his hands slid under her, lifting her slightly. Inside her, he hit a spot that made her hips rock and it felt like she was on a spaceship flying up, about to break through the fire-hot atmosphere. Jackson increased his pace and Hayley hurtled into another dimension, disintegrating as she hit that wall of pleasure.

Jackson pumped faster into her and she heard, sort of, his shout of pleasure, felt his body contract under her hands. While she attempted to find the scattered pieces of her body and soul, dismembered by her soul-shaking orgasm, he tensed and dug his fingers into her butt cheeks, before slumping on her, pushing her weight into her cushions.

Hayley turned her head and buried her face in his neck, breathing in the intoxicating concoction of his cologne, sex and pheromones. Lots and lots of pheromones.

She'd heard that sex could be addictive and now she, finally, knew why.

She was hooked.

Dammit.

* * *

It was Sunday morning, and Jackson was still asleep in her bed. Unfortunately, she wasn't on duty today so she didn't have the excuse to run out of the door…

Hayley had no idea what to do, how to handle the whole morning-after awkwardness.

Hayley stood in the doorway to her bedroom, shuffling from one foot to the other. The sex had been… *wow*…amazing, utterly mind-blowing. Jackson showed her how to enjoy her body, how to release her inhibitions, encouraged her to tell him what she liked—everything— and what she didn't—nothing.

Hayley felt like she'd attended a master class in making love, but class was over and she wasn't sure how to act.

Why wasn't there a handbook for these sorts of situations? And if there was, where did she find it?

"This isn't complicated, sweetheart." Jackson's growly voice drifted over to her. "You can either come back to bed or make coffee. I vote for the first."

Jackson lay on his stomach and Hayley's gaze fell on his broad back, her eyes tracing the indentation of his spine, the bunched muscles in his shoulder blades. Jackson took care of himself, of that there was no doubt.

"How do you keep in shape?" Hayley asked him.

Jackson cracked open one eye, yawned, and his eyelids drifted down again. "I run, swim, gym. Exercise is my way to combat stress." He rolled over, the sheet bunching tightly across his hips, showing an impressive amount of morning wood.

Yum.

Jackson pushed himself up into a seated position and ran his hands over his face. "God, I'm exhausted."

"Can't keep up with me, huh?" Hayley teased him. "You are a great deal older than me, you know."

"Come over here and I'll show you old," Jackson told her on a lazy grin. "And I'm sure it was you who told me that you couldn't come again, that you were too tired."

Hayley blushed. She had said that and she had been tired but then Jackson placed his mouth between her legs and had her begging for more.

She'd love to crawl back into his arms but she needed some space, some time to collect her thoughts and get her rampaging emotions under control.

Jackson ran a hand through his hair. "I like where your thoughts are going, Hayley, but maybe we should talk about last night."

Hayley wrinkled her nose. "Our fight?"

"Yeah. I'm not someone who sweeps things under the carpet, so let's clear the air." Jackson placed his hands behind his head and his biceps bulged. He looked like a cover model for an erotic romance novel and Hayley wanted to take a bite out of his big arms, to nibble on his neck.

She couldn't possibly think straight with him sitting there, naked under her covers, looking all scrumptious and kissable and well, fu—

"I'll meet you in the kitchen. And, depending on how that conversation goes, we can decide on how to spend the rest of the day," Jackson told her, tossing back the covers and standing up, gloriously naked and utterly unselfconscious. He didn't need to be. He was, frankly, beautiful in a way only a rugged, masculine man could be.

Hayley nodded, forced herself to turn away and, wearing just a tank top and a pair of panties, walked to her kitchen and put the kettle on the gas stove. After pulling mugs out of the cupboard, she spooned in coffee and impatiently waited for the water to boil.

If only she had some food in her empty fridge. She hadn't eaten anything last night and she could scarf an entire box of doughnuts.

The kettle started to whistle as Jackson walked into her kitchen, dressed in his tuxedo pants and his unbuttoned dress shirt.

He dropped into one of her mismatched chairs at her wobbly dining table and took the mug she held out to him. He sipped and grimaced. "God, this is…"

Hayley raised her eyebrows. "What's wrong with my coffee?"

Jackson took another sip and tried to hide his distaste. "It's…"

"Cheap," Hayley interjected, pulling out a chair and lifting her heels onto the seat. "I'm on a cop's salary, remember?"

Jackson tapped his finger against the handle of his mug. "Why is that, by the way? You're an heiress, the only daughter of one of the richest men in the state. Why aren't you working in Dallas, working in your dad's company, enjoying the Dallas social scene?"

Hayley pulled a face. "Can you see me working

crowds and fake smiling?" After sipping her coffee, she wrapped her arms around her bent legs. "That's exactly what they wanted me to do. I was supposed to go to college, do a degree in business marketing and run the PR side of Lopez Inc. My father had it all planned out, with all my brothers holding important positions in the company. He wanted me to join the family company, as well."

"And that wasn't what you wanted?"

Hayley sent him a scathing look. "No, I did not want to be their make-it-sound-pretty mouthpiece. I wanted to, I still want to, make a difference. I always wanted to study law and my father said he'd pay for my studies, provided I committed to working at the company, in PR and not in the legal department, for five years after I graduated, or until I got married and had kids."

Jackson's eyes flew upward. "Wow. That's pretty old-fashioned."

"My father is an old-fashioned guy." Hayley gathered her hair at the back of her head, twisted it into a knot and pulled it over one shoulder. "I told him to shove his offer and that I'd do it my way without his help."

Hayley picked up her mug and blew across the surface before taking a sip. "I know that he loves me and wants to protect me, but I will not let anyone dictate what I do and how I do it, not even my father." Hayley looked at Jackson, hoping he'd understand. "If I worked for my dad and with my brothers, I would be protected and cosseted, and have a firewall around me.

I needed to know if I could do it on my own, stand on my own two feet."

"Okay, but why did you become a cop?"

"After the blowup with my dad, I came to Royal—my grandparents lived here—and I managed to get a job as a dispatcher in the sheriff's department. Nate Battle helped me get into training. He hired me on the proviso that I keep studying.

"I grew up privileged, Jackson, so privileged, and I want to make a difference. I want to give back. It's important to me. Look, we all know that Royal has a lot of wealthy residents. But beyond the big mansions and the ranching and the independent shops, some people live close to the breadline, lots can't find permanent work. Thousands of immigrants live in fear of deportation and there's a growing problem with drugs and gangs. These problems are easy to ignore but I see and meet with the people who are faced with those realities and I try to help. I *need* to help. I can't turn a blind eye."

Jackson leaned back and stretched out his long legs. "I admire your drive and your ambition, Hayley."

And here it came, the criticism. "But?"

"But you need to be able to read the room, sweetheart," Jackson suggested. Because his tone lacked the bossiness and annoyance from the night before, Hayley's hackles didn't fly up.

"What do you mean?"

"I understand why you wanted to talk to Rafael. Something about him being mentioned in Arielle's diary?"

Hayley nodded.

"Okay, so if you'd taken the time to get some background intel on Rafael, you'd know that last night was the first time he set foot in Royal since he was seventeen. He and his father, Tobias, have a very strained relationship, one which Cammie and I would like to see repaired." Jackson pushed his still-full coffee cup away. "Rafe is also the type of guy who takes his responsibilities very seriously. Firstly, he would never put himself in the position of fathering a child, but if that pregnancy happened, he would never, ever abandon his child. Your accusation—"

"I didn't accuse him of anything," Hayley hotly replied.

"Fair point," Jackson said, placing his forearms on the kitchen table, "but you questioning him in such a public setting raised questions and started rumors. Those rumors might be enough to make Rafe leave Royal."

Hayley pulled a face. "Isn't that a little, well, cowardly to be chased out of town by a few words?"

Jackson's hard eyes nailed her to her chair. "You weren't there to see the wounds that were inflicted on him so you can't judge his actions, Hayley."

Hayley winced, acknowledging the hit. "You're right, I wasn't." She still didn't think she'd done anything wrong last night. "I asked him a simple question, Jackson. Did he know the Martin sisters or not? The rumor was not my fault and it was unfair of you to accuse me of that."

Jackson stared at her and finally nodded. "You're right, I was out of line."

Judging by Jackson's lack of enthusiasm, he hated apologizing almost as much as she did. God, they were a pair.

But he had a point about gathering intel before she dived into a situation. "But I hear you on reading the room. I'll try to do better in the future. I can't promise but I will try."

The corners of Jackson's mouth lifted. "Good enough."

Hayley looked at his satisfied expression and hoped that Jackson didn't think that he had her under control because he'd made her beg, weep and scream with pleasure and because she'd conceded this particular battle. She didn't want him to think that she would always be this easy to deal with because she frequently wasn't.

"I don't take orders well, Jackson."

"Yeah, I know. You've made that abundantly clear."

Hayley waggled her index finger between them. "I don't want you to think that anything has changed between us because I slept with you and because I was reasonable about your friend."

"What are you trying to say, Hayley?"

Hayley pushed aside her jumbled thoughts. "You were angry last night, but I got the feeling that not all of that anger was directed at me. I think it's fair to say that you overreacted, especially since I'm not your wife or even a girlfriend. So, what's up with that?"

Jackson took so long answering that Hayley didn't know if he would. "I like you, Hayley. I love your balls-to-the-wall attitude and I admire your ambition. I love making love to you—"

"But?"

Jackson hesitated again and Hayley wanted to shove her hand in his mouth and yank the words off his tongue.

"But you're not what I need, or want, long-term."

His words stung, a lot more than they should. Pride had her pushing her shoulders back and lifting her chin. "Damn, and here I thought you were about to offer me marriage."

Jackson looked a little green at the thought.

"Relax, Jackson, I'm not looking for anything long-term, either."

And she wasn't. She had things to do and goals to achieve. Work and studying and finding little Micah's father. But any girl in her position would feel a little, well, pissed off at his blunt words.

"That being said, would you mind telling me why I am such a bad bet?" Hayley's tone was polite but she was pretty sure Jackson wouldn't miss the underlying sarcasm.

Jackson stood up and wrapped his fingers around the back strut of the dining chair. "What do you know about my mother?"

"I know that she died when you were young. More than that, nothing."

"She didn't die. She left my dad and me," Jackson explained. His voice was devoid of emotion but his eyes reflected his distress. They were dark blue pools of unwanted memories, unresolved hurt and a whole lot of anger. "I saw her occasionally when I was a teenager but I haven't spoken to her since I was eighteen. I think she's still in New York City."

Wow. That was a long time to be estranged.

"My mom was, is, incredibly smart and ambitious. She was a Wall Street trader when she met my dad. When she got pregnant with me, my dad persuaded her to marry him and to move to Royal.

"She was miserable and she hated her life here in Royal. And, to an extent, she hated me because I was the reason she sacrificed her career, left the city, lost out on making a pile of money."

Hayley lowered her feet to the floor and watched Jackson pace her small kitchen. "She told you that?"

"I heard their yelling. She never wanted to be a mom, to be married. She wanted to be free to live her life on her terms. God, she was stubborn and so damn independent."

Ah, the dots she needed to connect were flashing like Christmas lights. "And you think I'm like her?"

Jackson's miserable expression was answer enough. "She was headstrong and thoughtless, completely convinced that she was right. You're not as hard as her but you are as ambitious, as willful."

"You didn't answer my question," Hayley stated, wondering why she was pushing him. Was she trying to drive a wedge between them because he scared her, emotionally? Because she knew that becoming involved with a man like Jackson, *with* Jackson, would mean having her wings clipped, being grounded, unable to be wholly herself?

Was she looking for a way to extract herself or to protect herself? Both?

"I like you, I do, but…long-term? We're oil and water."

Hayley nodded. "You're controlling and I'm uncontrollable.

"You want someone who is biddable and placid," Hayley added, surprised at the bitterness in her voice. She knew that theirs was a physical connection but the idea of not being what Jackson wanted hurt her, far more than it should.

"I saw what the fights and the arguments did to my dad, how he drew in on himself, how he second-guessed himself all the time. I vowed never to give a woman that much power over me, ever. And if I ever commit to a woman, which I doubt will happen, she'll be easy-going, someone who'd stand by my side and not compete with me."

She won't be you…

Hayley heard his unspoken words and added a few of her own. Jackson wanted someone who wasn't ambitious, who wasn't forthright, someone to stand in the shadows while he absorbed all the sunlight. Growing up in her family, she'd been pushed toward the shade, told that the light was too bright for her, that she had no place there.

If she married, if she ever even committed to someone, she'd choose someone who'd allow her to stand in her own beam of sunlight, someone who would help her fly to the sun, not keep her away from it.

It was obvious that Jackson wasn't, and never would be, that person.

And the realization made her profoundly sad.

Hayley rolled her coffee mug between the palms of her hands, thinking about how to extract herself from this conversation with as much grace as possible. Unfortunately, grace wasn't one of her strongest qualities.

She forced a smile onto her face and lifted her head. "Well, good thing I only want to have fun with your body, Michaels."

Jackson released the grip on his chair and flexed his fingers. He stared at her as if trying to read her thoughts. "So, you'd be prepared to do this again, without strings and expectations?"

Honestly, she'd far prefer to kick him out, tell him to go to hell and lick her wounds but her damn pride wouldn't let him think that he'd hurt her, even a little bit.

She didn't want a relationship, especially one with an alpha male like Jackson, so why was she feeling a little emotionally battered and bruised?

"Let's play that by ear," Hayley told him, standing up. She glanced down at her tank top and wished that she was wearing more clothes. This wasn't the type of conversation one should have half-naked.

Jackson stared at her, searching her face for something, but Hayley kept her smile on her face, refusing to show him that she was upset.

Would anyone, ever, just love her for who she was, warts and all?

It seemed not.

Hayley forced herself to move toward him, to stand on her tiptoes to drop a kiss on the corner of his mouth. "Thanks for a fun night. I'm going to shower while you get dressed. Please flip the lock on the front door on your way out." Hayley walked away and she was about to step into the hallway when Jackson said her name.

Hayley slowly turned and lifted her eyebrows.

"I…" Jackson rubbed his hands over his face. When he dropped them, she saw the confusion on his face.

Good. Being kept off-balance would probably do him the world of good. "I'll see you around," he finally said, buttoning his shirt.

"See you around," Hayley blithely responded, concentrating on not bolting from the room.

Seven

Jackson drove away, his gaze frequently returning to the rearview mirror to look at the silly, shades-of-purple house.

Oil and water...

Wanting control and being uncontrollable...

Jackson steered his car around the corner, Hayley's whimsical house fading from view.

They'd both used the right words, said what they needed to, and now they both knew where they stood. They might, or might not, hook up again in the future, but there was no chance of a deeper connection forming between them.

They were on the same page...

But Jackson couldn't help thinking that the conversation had hurt Hayley, that she was hiding her pain behind her tough-girl facade. He'd caught flickers of anguish in her eyes, seen it in the tightening of her lips, the tension in her shoulders.

And the thought of someone hurting her—even if that someone was him—made him feel sick to his stomach. Nobody was allowed to do that, especially not him.

Jackson braked and considered spinning his car around and heading back to her house to apologize, or grovel, or to kiss her hurt away.

Pulling over to the side of the road, he rested his forehead on the steering wheel, wishing he didn't want her so much, that he could stop thinking about her.

He'd told the truth when he said that he liked her. He did. He enjoyed her sharp mind, her sassy mouth, her independent spirit.

He adored her body, loved hearing the sounds she made as he pleasured her...

Their bodies fit together like they were carved from the same jigsaw pattern. She was soft where he was hard, her skin silky smooth and scented. Sliding into her felt like coming home...

But these were, undoubtedly, the same feelings his dad felt on first meeting his mother. The chemistry between them had been, so he'd heard, electric.

Their fights had been equally combustible...

Jackson lifted his head and flexed his cramping fingers, annoyed that this woman, so much younger than him, could tie him up in so many knots. He hadn't given anyone this much headspace since high school and he didn't like it.

Hayley Lopez was not going to derail his perfectly ordered, smooth-sailing, calm life. He was perfectly content with charting his course, adjusting the sails when the wind changed, and he liked not having to ask anyone's opinion on how and when to do that.

Jackson did not doubt that Hayley, like his mother, would try to take the helm.

Jackson started his car and pulled off, wondering if he was being fair comparing Hayley to his mom. Yes, they were both driven and ambitious but Hayley wasn't as intractable as his mom, not really. After their tempers cooled—extinguished by incredible sex—she'd considered his viewpoint and conceded as much as she could. His mom would never admit to being wrong or to making a mistake and had been convinced of her moral and intellectual superiority in every situation.

His mom didn't know how to capitulate, to back down or to apologize. Hayley, it seemed, did.

Hayley might be ambitious and forthright but she wasn't cruel or selfish. Her desire to make a difference, to change people's lives, was on display for anyone to see.

His mom had been the ultimate victim, convinced that life had handed her a terrible hand. According to her, because of her pregnancy and marriage, she'd been deprived of the job promotions, the huge salary and the year-end bonuses. Despite being married to a billionaire, she felt that the only money that counted was the money she made, the only opinion that mattered was hers.

His mom had been a classic narcissist and the ultimate control freak.

Hayley was a strong woman, he knew that, but she wasn't a selfish monster.

But that didn't matter. Nothing mattered but his need to keep her at arm's distance, to not allow himself to feel more for her than he should. He'd loved his mom, as much as she allowed him to, but her leaving had been a relief for him and complete devastation for his dad. He'd watched his father's heart break, and he would never allow that to happen to him.

Hayley Lopez, young, gorgeous and determined, might just have the power to do that to him so he needed to put an enormous amount of distance, physical and emotional, between them.

He knew what he needed to do but never expected it to be this hard.

A few days later, in his man cave—a separate building to the left of his lap pool—Jackson sat at his custom-made poker table and pushed a pile of chips toward the center and lifted his beer bottle to his lips. Brett scowled at him and glanced at the cards in his hands before tossing his cards facedown on the green baize.

"You suck, Michaels," Brett told him as Jackson raked the chips toward him, adding to his very impressive total. Brett Harston, along with Nate Battle, Daniel Clayton and Clint Rockwell, were his poker opponents tonight but that could change next week, depending on who was around and available.

Clint dealt another hand and Jackson looked around

his man cave, remembering that his father used to hold monthly poker games in this room twenty-five-plus years ago. Back then it used to be a storeroom attached to the pool house. His dad and buddies sat at plastic tables and pulled bottles out of an ice chest because Hazel hadn't approved of his gambling and refused to allow his childhood friends, and their smelly cigars, into the house.

Jackson knocked down the old pool house years ago and directed his designer to create a man cave of epic proportions. The long room, with a wall of glass looking out onto the pool, hot tub and landscaped garden, held a six-man poker table, a bar and a hundred-year-old billiard table.

Two pinball machines sat at the back of the room, sandwiching an old jukebox. The first deer his dad ever shot—relegated to a storage room because his mom hated it—was affixed to the end wall, a University of Texas scarf wound around its neck.

He loved this room. It was one of his favorites in his extensive mansion on the outskirts of Royal and he loved it best when it was filled with his close friends and cigar smoke.

Clint picked up his cards and moved them around. "How's the Stone Lake development progressing?" he asked.

Jackson saw that he held two aces and not much else. "It isn't," he answered Clint. "Most of the owners have expressed a willingness to sell but I can't do anything until Bubba agrees to sell his land. His property is the centerpiece of the development and without it I might as well shelve the entire project."

"Is that what you are thinking of doing?" Nate Battle asked him, leaning back in his chair.

Jackson shrugged. "Bubba won't sell so I might as well." It burned his ass to walk away from such an exciting project and he genuinely thought it was a good development for Royal. Apart from the work it would bring in, there was a shortage of property and he'd fulfill that need.

"He's a stubborn old goat," Nate commented.

"Not helped by your deputy who keeps telling him not to sell until he's good and ready. And that Royal doesn't need a development at Stone Lake."

Nate grinned at his sour words. "Officer Lopez is entitled to give an old man her opinion if he asks for it," he calmly replied.

"She gives everyone her opinion all the time," Jackson grumbled.

"Hayley isn't scared to wade in," Nate said. "With three bossy brothers and a very controlling father, she's had to defend her corner."

"Who's met her father?" Jackson asked, knowing he was opening himself up to being ragged on by his friends.

"Why? Are you trying to figure out how to ask him permission to date her?" Daniel demanded, his eyes filled with amusement. Daniel was one of his oldest friends and, like the others, lived to rag on him.

"As if," Jackson retorted. "She's too young and…" Too sexy, and too intriguing and too smart and…

Shit.

"I've met Juan Lopez," Nate said, tossing his cards away. "His parents owned a holiday cottage on Stone Lake when Hayley was a kid. She spent a lot of time with her grandparents, especially over the summer holidays. Her parents also used to visit for two weeks every July."

"I heard that Juan was hard and demanding and has, or had, a hell of a chip on his shoulder. He kept those kids on a short leash," Brett stated. "All hearsay. I barely know the guy."

Nate picked the label off his bottle, his expression pensive. "I think that's what he wants people to see. In Juan's mind, people respect a man who is strong and tough. I'm not sure that's who he really is…"

His cards forgotten, Jackson leaned forward, intrigued at this window into Hayley's life. "What do you mean?"

Nate thought for a minute before speaking. "One summer, the Lopez boys were teenagers, the oldest must've been sixteen, so Hayley must've been about ten. I caught them car surfing—"

"What's that?" Clint asked.

"It's where one person gets on top of the car and holds on while someone else drives the car down the dirt road, trying to fishtail them off," Daniel explained.

He and Dan were once the undisputed kings of car surfing. "Standard small-town fun," Jackson said.

"But still dangerous," Nate said. "But I did it and hundreds of teenagers before and after me did it and

I've never heard of anyone getting hurt." He shrugged. "But God protects the stupid.

"Anyway, I caught them. Hayley was in the back seat, her eyes as wide as saucers. I pulled them over and did what we always do—"

"Handcuff the perps, threaten to take them to jail and lecture them before calling the parents," Jackson interrupted Nate, remembering his encounter with a Royal sheriff's deputy. These days, certain members of the force were a lot prettier and filled out their uniforms a lot better.

"I did all that and their old man arrived at the scene," Nate continued. "When the boys told him that I'd threatened to take them to jail, Lopez told me to lock them up for the night."

Jackson lowered his beer bottle, astounded. "Was he being serious?"

"Nah, he was just trying to scare some sense into them.

"Lopez lined them up in a row and started rattling off in Spanish. He tore fifty strips off them, telling them that they disgraced his name, embarrassed themselves, how disappointed he was in them. I watched them shrink in on themselves and thought that he was what everybody said he was…a hard man with huge expectations and little room for compromise."

Nate smiled. "Then Hayley, her hair in two braids, started yelling at her father, telling him that he was being unreasonable, that her brothers were just having some fun. I'll never forget that kid, so full of fire, standing up for her much-older brothers."

Jackson could see it. Hayley, when faced with in-justice, would always wade into the fight.

"She and her father got into it and Hayley refused to back down."

Interesting, Jackson thought. That went a little way to explain Hayley's tough-girl, I'm-good-on-my-own attitude. When one grew up in a tough environment, one could either bend with the wind, ride out the storm or face it head-on.

"In the middle of arguing with Hayley, Juan threw up his hands, walked off the road and disappeared be-hind a bush. I was standing off to the side, could see him, and the guy bent over and tossed his cookies. When he stood up straight, I could see that he was shaking, and was as white as a sheet," Nate explained. "It hit me he was bone-deep terrified of something happening to his kids, and that, maybe, he was such a hard-ass because he loved them to distraction.

"I think Hayley was his favorite kid by a country mile," Nate added. "When she was defending her broth-ers, he looked almost bemused, like he was trying to figure out where she came from. When she stomped off to the car, he smiled, and I saw the love and pride in his eyes. To my mind, that kid was—probably still is—the reason the sun rose and set for him."

"But she left home at eighteen, and doesn't have much to do with her family," Jackson countered.

"Probably because she's as stubborn and contrary as her old man and won't allow anyone to tell her what to do. They might not talk much, but there's love there," Nate replied.

Lots to think about, Jackson thought as he inspected the cards he was dealt. He started to ask Nate another question about Hayley and realized he was opening himself up to a round of ragging and a great deal of speculation.

No, his questions could wait until he got Nate alone or—here was an idea—ask Hayley herself. After a few minutes of trash talking each other about their shitty hands, Brett returned to the original subject of his dead-in-the-water development. "So, are you going to dump the project?"

"Probably," Jackson replied, resting his forearms on the table. "The hand I'm holding isn't good. Bubba has an emotional attachment to the land. His sons and wife are buried there—"

"I'd forgotten that," Nate said, nodding.

"—and he places a lot of stock in Hayley's opinion." Jackson grimaced. "I can't afford to waste any more time and energy on something that probably won't fly."

"Years ago, I remember a proposal coming up before the city council to build a bike, jogging and walking path in that area," Daniel said before taking a sip from the glass of red wine at his elbow.

"We need something like that in Royal," Brett agreed.

"We do and Stone Lake is a pretty venue," Clint agreed. Of course it was pretty, Jackson thought. He wouldn't build a multimillion-dollar development in a dump.

"The residents would love it, especially if someone established a restaurant at the site, built boat ramps and Jet Ski launches and developed a picnic area," Dan added.

Jackson saw that all eyes were on him and he squirmed in his chair, waiting for someone to spit it out.

Clint was the one who found his balls first. "You should build that, Jack."

"No profit in it," Jack automatically replied.

"You are wealthy enough to forgo the profit on this one project, Michaels."

Jackson squirmed under Nate's hard look. Yeah, he was. Of course he was. If he never raised another building again, he had enough to last him several lifetimes.

"A project like the one Dan is suggesting would generate a lot of goodwill, and weren't you looking for a way to honor your dad? You could name the venture and venue after him," Nate suggested. A sneaky smile crossed his face. "And it would get a certain woman off your back."

He'd far prefer to have her on *her* back… *Focus, Michaels.*

Jackson tipped his chair back so that it rested on its two back feet and looked at the ceiling and considered the suggestion. He already owned a few properties around Stone Lake, pieces of undeveloped land he'd either snapped up years ago or inherited from his dad. It wouldn't take much to convert the land into picnic areas, to build boat ramps and, possibly, buildings to house a casual restaurant.

It was an idea…one he needed to give a lot more thought.

Jackson dropped his chair down and picked up his

cards. He saw that his friends were waiting for him to speak, and he shook his head.

"I'll think about it," he told them. He looked from one trusted face to the other, keeping his scowl on his face. "Do not breathe a word about this to anyone. If someone hears about this idea, the town will take it and run with it and I do not need to be harassed by the Royal Reporters or the general public."

His friends nodded and Jackson knew that nobody would breathe a word. His friends were crap poker players, but they knew how to keep their mouths shut.

A month later Hayley, sitting in her patrol car a half mile down from Bubba's driveway at Stone Lake, yawned and tried to keep her eyes from fluttering closed. It was Saturday but she was on duty, huddled into her car on a chilly fall day. She'd had a hell of a week, frustrating, annoying and unexciting.

Eve was still in the hospital getting her heart checked out, Sierra was still researching the story of the child abandoned over a century ago, Micah was still living with Cammie and she'd made no progress to find the baby's real father. Rafael Wentworth was in town but refused to talk to her or anyone from the Royal sheriff's department. She was late with two assignments and her professor was getting antsy.

In law enforcement parlance, her week had been a shit show.

Oh, and her mother was demanding her presence at her always over-the-top Thanksgiving dinner in Dallas. Hayley would far prefer to spend the day eating junk food and binge-watching Netflix.

But she'd skipped Thanksgiving last year and made only a brief appearance for Christmas, skipped Easter and ducked out of their Fourth of July party with a have-to-work excuse.

If she told her mother she wouldn't be home for Thanksgiving, she could expect a SWAT team to haul her back home.

She could push her mother only so far...

She'd also spent too much time thinking about Jackson, wondering when he would be back in town. Before he left Royal over a week ago, they'd managed to have dinner twice, and to catch a movie once—always ending the night with earth-moving sex. In between their "dates," they'd also snuck in a few late-night, hot-as-hell hookups.

Despite her outwardly casual attitude, Hayley felt branded by him, like it would take her a long, long time to move on from him. If she ever could.

There was something about him that her entire being—heart, body and soul—responded to. He was the first man who'd not only made her body sing and her soul sigh but he seemed to, on a cellular level, get her. Something about him made her think that if she could break down her wall around her heart and hand it to him, he'd take care of it.

That was if he wanted to.

Which he didn't.

As a result, she was, as she was every day, feeling horny and irritable and the emotions had yet to dissipate. Knowing she wasn't fit to be around people, she routinely volunteered for the horrible jobs that would take her, and her bad mood, away from her colleagues and out of the public eye. So far this week, she'd searched for records in the dusty basement, driven to Dallas to deliver a packet of evidence that needed to be forensically examined and spent time on the computer updating their records.

This morning, knowing that her serotonin levels were still low, she'd volunteered to monitor one of the more desolate back roads into Royal for two hours, in a ridiculous attempt to do vehicle checks and catch speedsters. Nate just shook his head and told her not to look at any dairy cows as she might curdle their milk.

Her boss thought he was a comedian.

But, in his way, Nate was looking out for her. He knew that the traffic on this back road was minimal and in the half hour she'd been here, she hadn't seen one passing car. Being stuck on the side of the road also gave her a couple of hours to do some work, to catch up on her assignments. And that's what she'd intended to do but thoughts of Jackson kept strolling into her brain, plopping down and making themselves comfortable. She remembered the way his lips curved against her skin, his big hand running down her hip, his delightful belly button and his equally delightful...

Hayley was jerked out of her sexy daydream by someone tapping on her half-opened window and her hand instantly flew to the handle of her weapon, pulling it out and up and into...

Jackson's face.

Perfect.

Jackson pushed away the barrel with one finger, the anger in his eyes unmistakable. Hayley couldn't blame him. She wouldn't want a gun in her face, either. Hayley placed her weapon in her lap, rubbed her hands over her face and finally looked into Jackson's still-angry face.

"You scared me," Hayley told him, her tone fractious. "You shouldn't sneak up on me."

Jackson opened her door and gestured her to get out. When she was on her feet, he pointed at his enormous pickup truck. "It weighs two tons and isn't quiet. You were zoned out. Jesus, Hayley, you are a sheriff's deputy! What the hell were you thinking?"

That I miss you, that I want to be with you.

"Sweetheart, this is the second time I've caught you unaware. You got to know that you put yourself in danger when you don't pay attention to your surroundings. And that scares me," he told her, sounding annoyingly reasonable.

She wanted to argue with him, she did, but she didn't have a leg to stand on. She'd messed up. "Are you going to tell Nate about this?"

"No, I'm not a snitch. But you can't keep doing this. Why are you doing this? What are you doing here? Why weren't you paying attention?"

She heard the worry in his voice and sighed. Hayley left her car and rested her butt against the back passenger door, crossing her arms. "I'm here because I have an attitude problem. I have had one all week."

Jackson looked around. "But why here?"

"Nate knows that it's an empty stretch of road, that I'm behind in my assignments and that being here is a good chance for me to catch up."

"Yet you weren't working when I arrived," Jackson pointed out. "I see no open books, no laptop."

Hayley lifted her chin and her eyes slammed into his. "No, I was thinking about you and what you did to me and how much I wish you'd do it to me again."

He stared at her, the blue in his eyes deeper and darker than ever before. He raised his hand and clasped her face, his thumb sliding across her bottom lip. "I haven't stopped thinking about you, either."

"You said that this can't work, that it won't work," Hayley pointed out.

"It won't. But that doesn't mean that I've stopped lusting after you."

Oh, man, she wished he wouldn't say things like that. Words like that made her think of his mouth on hers, his hand on her breast or down the back, or the front of her pants.

"Can you take a break from your busy schedule of thinking?" Jackson asked.

Hayley heard both amusement and a trace of sarcasm in his voice. She glanced at her watch, saw that it was close to lunchtime and nodded. Picking up her radio, she told the dispatcher that she was taking a break and would return to duty in an hour. "I'm just going to take a walk by Stone Lake, clear my head."

"Copy that, Lopez."

Hayley looked at Jackson. "I'm off duty for the next hour or so. What are you thinking?"

"Many, many things," Jackson replied. He looked down the deserted road, then up. "How many cars have used this road this morning?"

"None," Hayley told him. "Most of the cabins out this way are holiday cottages and are all currently empty. Of the year-round residents, only Bubba uses this road and his car is in the shop. So, no, I'm not expecting a lot of action on this superbusy highway."

Jackson's expression held a hint of daring. "Want to do something?"

There was something in his tone, in the quirk of his lips, that had her skin tingling and her nipples tightening. "Like what?"

Jackson took her hand, led her to the passenger side of his car. He opened the two passenger doors, back and front, and Hayley realized that the tall doors made a little cage, and no passing traffic could see what they were doing.

Not that she was expecting anyone on this lonely road.

Jackson rested his forearm on the vehicle above her head and stared down at her. Hayley knew what he wanted and God, she wanted it to.

"I could get fired, Jackson."

"For indulging in a kiss on the side of an empty road while you're off duty? I don't think so," Jackson responded, nuzzling the side of her mouth. "I've missed you, Hayley. I've wanted you in my bed and my arms every night since leaving you."

"You know that we can't be—"

Jackson covered her mouth with a quick, hard, toe-curling kiss. "I don't know what we can or can't be. All I know is that I need to kiss you, to have you kiss me back."

When he put it like that, she couldn't say no. Hayley peeled her hands off the truck and placed them on his chest, slowly moving them up to his shoulders and around to the back of his neck. "You confuse and frustrate me but when I'm with you, I can't think," Hayley told him.

"Well, then don't think, just feel."

Okay, then.

Jackson shivered when Hayley's fingers speared into his hair and her tongue wound around his. His cock hardened, pulsed, but instead of anticipating what was to come—and there was no way he was taking her on the side of a country road—he sank into the passion, allowing it to flow over him, letting each wave go. For now, he was content to explore her mouth, to run his thumb up and down her slender throat, to inhale the citrus scent of her body lotion. Stepping closer, Jackson felt her breasts push into his chest, his erection into her stomach, and his breath hitched and his heart stuttered. This woman, the way she felt, smelled, kissed, touched… He was addicted to her.

Jackson pulled her bottom lip between his teeth and nibbled gently before lifting his mouth off hers, needing to look into her dark, fabulous eyes, struck by the thought that it was no coincidence that he'd found Hayley on the side of the road. He was starting to think that he'd always find her, that his heart and body would always want and need to know where she was and what she was doing.

He was also starting to accept that he was put on this earth to pleasure Hayley. That making love to her was what he was best at. Promising himself that he wouldn't take this too far, he skimmed his hands over her body, frustrated by her jacket and the thick material of her uniform. With growing impatience, Jackson unzipped her puffy jacket and immediately went to work on the buttons of her shirt until he had enough space to slide his hand inside and cover her breast with his palm. Needing to taste her, he pulled her bra cup away and swiped his tongue over her nipple, reveling in her sexy moans. He felt the weak sun on his shoulders, heard the sound of a distance *killy!* call of a kestrel.

As long as he didn't hear the sound of an engine or tractor, he was good…

"You are so perfect, so sexy. I've missed you so much."

"Jackson…"

Jackson pulled her shirt out of her pants, undid her button and eased her zipper down. A slight breeze picked up as his fingers skated over her muscled stomach, under her panties and down into her strip of hair, parting her folds, finding her heat. Hayley groaned his name as his fingers probed her, his thumb caressing her nub of nerves, making her shake.

"Open your legs a little, Hayley-mine," Jackson gruffly told her, smiling when she immediately obeyed his instruction. Hayley didn't take orders but when he touched her, she was more than happy to comply.

When she got more confident in herself and in her lovemaking skills, that would change. And God, he hoped he'd be around to be the one taking orders instead of giving them.

He couldn't think of anything hotter...

Jackson slid his middle finger into her, then another, and Hayley stiffened, caught up in her pleasure. His cock was hard and ready to rock and roll but that wouldn't happen. This was all about her.

"This is madness, Jackson. What are we doing?"

"If you don't know, then I'm doing it wrong," Jackson told her, smiling.

Jackson tapped a spot deep inside her and Hayley's fingernails lodged themselves in the muscle of his shoulders, perfect pinpricks of pain.

"Am I making you smile yet, sweetheart? Banishing your blues?"

Hayley looked heated and harassed, exactly like a woman on the edge of orgasm should. "You're driving me insane, Michaels."

Hayley moved her hand, skimming his lower abdomen to find his hard cock. She palmed him and Jackson hauled in a harsh breath, wishing he could strip her down, wind her legs around his waist and plunge.

Her hand on him, her thumb rubbing his length, tempted him to do exactly that so Jackson picked up her hand and told her to keep it flat against the vehicle.

"If you don't, I'll stop," he warned her, brushing his thumb against her clitoris.

Hayley had just enough gumption, enough sass left to toss her head and lift her chin. "Then stop. I can cope."

He played with her clit again and spread his fingers wide inside her and smiled at her deep whimper. "You sure about that, Hayley? Do you want me to stop?"

Hayley shook her head but her eyes remained defiant. Needing her capitulation, needing to know that she wanted him and his touch, Jackson lifted his other hand to grip her jaw. "Tell me what you want, Hayley."

Jackson saw Hayley's attempt to remain unaffected, but within a few seconds her defiance disappeared and lust, animalistic and uncontrollable, flashed in her eyes, skimmed across her face. "I want you inside me, I want your mouth on my breasts and I want to come."

"I can't be inside you but I can give you this."

Jackson increased the friction on her clit, pumped his finger, and Hayley whimpered into his neck and begged for release. She dropped her face to place her mouth on the bare patch of skin between his open collar and his throat, sucking on his skin, panting in pleasure as he mimicked the sex act with his fingers. She arched her back, demanded that he kiss her, but Jackson wanted to watch her as she disintegrated in his arms, wanting to see if she could look even more beautiful than she already did.

Hayley's eyes closed and he knew she'd stepped into the world he'd taken her to, lost in the way he made her feel. He was a guy in his midthirties. He'd had many lovers, probably too many, but none were as responsive as Hayley. None of them made him want to forgo his pleasure to make her feel desired, lovely, indescribably feminine and a little wicked.

He'd always remember this moment. How the wind

pulled tendrils of her dark hair from her tidy bun, the way her eyelashes rested on her cheek, the soft sounds she made as she climbed higher and higher. The weak sunlight, the sound of the wind in the trees, the smell of dust and citrus and Hayley's light perfume.

Jackson pulled back farther to look at Hayley, noticing that she was close, about to lose herself to pleasure. He stilled his hand, wanting her to wait, needing to watch her a little longer, to see her brown-black eyes widen, the way pleasure danced over her skin, painting it with a pink sheen.

He kissed her mouth, needing the connection, the intimacy of the act. Because kissing was intimate, sometimes even more so than sex itself.

Hayley writhed and her moans became louder and her demand for release more intense. Pulling his fingers out, he pushed them back into her slick channel and dropped to his knees to cover her clit with his mouth, teasing the bud with his tongue.

Hayley released a loud yell as she bucked against him and he felt her channel clench around his fingers, her fingers pulling his hair as she bucked against his mouth. She banged her head against the car, once, twice, her pants splitting the silence of the country air.

After a minute, maybe more, her breathing slowed and she relaxed, softly murmuring his name. Jackson stood up and, after gently pulling her pants up and closing her zipper, knew that for as long as he lived, he'd always remember Hayley standing in the space between his car doors, the rays of the sun deepening the golden tint of her skin, her ugly uniform covering her gorgeous curves. Her hair was half falling from her bun but her lips were curved with feminine satisfaction. Best of all, under his hands, she still vibrated from the violent orgasm that he'd given her.

He didn't want to move, to break the spell.

So they stood there for a while, her one hand on his hip, her other hand still resting against the door, her head tilted to the side, their eyes locked. Then Hayley moved and she wrapped her arms around his neck and buried her face in his neck, her lips on his skin.

It was curiously intimate, strangely and compellingly sexy, standing on the side of the road in the middle of the day with a woman whom he had no business wanting, her body tucked into his.

This mattered. She mattered.

And he didn't know where to go from here.

Eight

Sitting in her car, Hayley watched the dust that Jackson's car kicked up dissipate, trying to make sense of the last twenty minutes. The facts were undisputed: Jackson had rocketed her to an orgasm on the side of the road during her lunch break.

Hayley released a loud groan and dropped her forehead against her steering wheel. She was pretty sure that their little tryst was totally against regulations and that if anyone found out, Nate would fire her ass.

Breathe, Hayley. No one had passed them, she didn't intend to divulge any information and Jackson wasn't the type to kiss and tell.

But the fact remained that she'd taken a hell of a risk. Should this get out, she could lose her job.

What the hell had she been thinking?

She hadn't been and that was the problem. Whenever Jackson Michaels was near, her brain shut down and her libido took control and made her act like a feral, wild woman. What was it about this man who could upend her entire world?

His looks aside—and they were great looks and an even better body—she liked the man. She liked his sly sense of humor, his decisiveness, his way of cutting through frivolities to get to the heart of the matter. She liked his loyalty to his friends and family, his honesty and his forthright way of speaking; she always knew where she stood with Jackson.

He was strong and sensible, ferociously intelligent. He was ambitious but he wasn't egocentric. He was also demanding and bossy and commanding, but having more than a fair share of those negative traits herself, she didn't hold his flaws against him. Their age difference was irrelevant. Guys her age were, well, annoying. They were still, for the most part, trying to find themselves, were insecure or conceited, and mostly irritating.

She preferred the company of older men, always had, and she loved being with Jackson more than anyone else.

Hayley lifted her head off the steering wheel and picked up her water bottle, taking a long sip. Wow, she was thinking of the *L* word, considering the concept. She didn't know what falling in love or being addicted to someone felt like but if it meant not being able to stop thinking about Jackson, wishing she were with him, needing to connect with him, then there was a good chance that she was there.

No, no, no! She didn't want to be, *couldn't be*, in love with him. It was too soon, they hadn't spent enough time together, hardly scratched the surface of what made each other tick.

And she had things to do, her job, people to help, a life to create, a law degree to complete. She did not need the distraction of a man in her life.

And, let's not forget that she was exactly the type of woman Jackson didn't want and wasn't looking for. He'd stated his preferences. He wanted someone placid and easy-going. She was mouthy, in your face and assertive. As his girlfriend, he'd expect her to toe the line and not rock the boat, but that wasn't her style. Hell, at eighteen, she'd defied her powerful and domineering father and she would never regret making the break for freedom, for being in control of her own life.

She would not give up her independence for love. She couldn't. It wasn't part of her psyche.

She and Jackson might share combustive chemistry but, if this situation was a poker game, she was holding a pair of twos. He was attracted to her, but he couldn't deal with who she was, at her core. She was attracted to him and she refused to be someone she wasn't to be loved by him.

Rock, meet Hard Place.

On leaving her, Jackson told her to come to his place after work, no doubt to take up where they left off minutes ago. And yeah, she wanted to be with him, to love and be loved by him, but could she sleep with him, knowing that there could never be more between them than chemistry and desire? But the hell of it was that as soon as she saw Jackson, the minute she looked into his eyes—she didn't even need him to touch her—she'd start shedding her clothes. Or his clothes.

You're heading for heartbreak, Lopez, and you know it. You know that if you allow this thing between us to grow legs, to become brighter and bolder, that you will end up trying to glue together pieces of your broken heart. This is not going to end well, you know this.

Walk away now...

I can't...

Hayley slapped the steering wheel, feeling frustrated and impatient and confused. This wasn't who she was, what she did. She had goals and worked out what steps she needed to take to reach those goals. She was disciplined and thoughtful and determined and decisive.

Jackson made her feel like she was a turtle trying to swim its way through a lava flow. Scorched and bewildered and uncertain and scared.

Hayley cursed the burning sensation in her eyes and swallowed back the tears gathering in her throat. *Wonderful.* No man, ever—not even her father or the unfaithful cowboy—made her cry and she hated that Jackson could.

Hated wanting him so much, hated feeling like she was flying apart.

Hayley opened her glove box, pulled a tissue from the box inside and wiped her eyes, calling herself a fool for being weepy. She blew her nose, breathed deeply and tried to pull herself together.

So far today, she'd accomplished less than nothing. Her assignment was untouched, the road was empty of traffic and she'd simply wasted a few hours. And that was unacceptable.

Thinking that she'd check on Bubba before heading back to the office, she started her engine and did a quick U-turn. She pushed her car faster over Bubba's pitted road than she should and pulled up in front of his cottage with its spectacular view of Stone Lake. Her father sold her grandparents' cottage after their deaths and Hayley deeply missed them and being able to hang out by the water.

She'd been happiest here, during those long summers she spent on the lake, boating and fishing.

Hayley exited her vehicle and called Bubba's name, wondering why the elderly man hadn't stepped onto his porch to greet her. Ignoring her little kick of worry, she climbed the steps of his porch and rapped on his door. When the older man didn't answer, she frowned. It was lunchtime and Bubba was always at home at this hour. His car was in the shop. She'd seen it there when she passed the other day. So where could he be?

Hayley walked around the corner of his wraparound porch and looked out onto the blue waters of the lake. It was too cold to swim now but she recalled swimming out to the red buoy that bobbed in the wind chopped water. Hayley saw a figure in the distance, squinted and recognized Bubba's hunched back, his whiter-than-snow hair. He was quite far down the rocky beach and it would take too long to walk to him so she decided to call him later to check on him.

Hayley walked back around to the front door and glanced down, frowning when she saw the white business card on the wooden plank. She picked up the card, her heart thumping when she saw Jackson's name under his company logo. Turning the card over, she frowned at his block print writing.

Bubba, the documents are ready to sign. Please contact me so that we can finalize this matter. JM.

What the hell?

Hayley stared down, not wanting to acknowledge the fact that he'd done it, he'd persuaded or, more likely, bullied Bubba into selling his property so that he could develop the area around Stone Lake.

That's where he'd been when he came across her on the side of the road. He'd been out here, wanting to talk to Bubba.

And, judging by his message, they'd struck a deal. Bubba hadn't called her or asked for her input or advice. And that hurt. It shouldn't but it did. Maybe she, or her legal skills, weren't needed in this town as much as she thought.

Her heart aching, Hayley placed the card on the small corner table, securing it with a ceramic pot holding a cactus with a pink flower.

Bubba's capitulation to Jackson, another win for corporate America, stung. Her lake was never going to be the same again. This vista would change and not for the good. And all because Jackson-damn-Michaels wanted another sprawling development with his name on it.

She couldn't possibly be in love with a man like him, a man who couldn't appreciate nature, who'd pestered an old man into finally selling his beloved property, who didn't care for the opinion of the community he lived in. She would not be in love with him. Any feelings stopped here, right now.

She was put-a-fork-in-her-done.

Hayley pulled her cell out of her jacket pocket and dialed his number, impatient for him to answer.

"Sweetheart, everything okay?"

Stupid heart for bouncing off her chest, crazy that her womb clenched at the sound of his voice. Her attraction to him was very damn inconvenient.

"Where are you now?" Hayley demanded, ignoring his question.

"At my house."

"Stay there, I'll be there in ten."

"Can't wait for later, huh?" Jackson purred, his voice deepening to a darker, sexier tone. It sent prickles up Hayley's spine and all over her skin, causing her to close her eyes.

"I've just showered but that shouldn't be a problem," Jackson murmured.

It took Hayley a while to make sense of his words and when she did, she blushed. And then the images of Jackson's strong hand on his shaft, his wet head tipped back to rest on the tiles, eyes closed as he pleasured himself, crashed over her and she had to place her hand on the wall of the house to steady herself.

That was an image she didn't need…

Hayley gritted her teeth, annoyed to feel the heat between her legs. "As I said, I'll be there in ten."

She made it seven and a half.

* * *

Hayley wasn't coming over to pick up where they left off.

Somehow, because life was a bitch, something had gone badly wrong in the half hour between his leaving her on the side of the road and her tense phone call.

Hell, would anything ever be easy with this woman?

Jackson dressed quickly and ran a towel over his wet hair, before raking it back with his fingers. He glanced in the mirror above his sleek credenza and grimaced at the crow's feet at his eyes, the grooves by the sides of his mouth, the flecks of gray he could see in his hair.

Thirty-six years old and he'd just taken an unexpected shower, spent some time with himself to take the edge off, to get through the day. No woman, ever, had forced him into an afternoon shower to find some relief. Insane that it was a twenty-three-, almost twenty-four-year-old who'd fractured his control.

There was something very wrong with this picture. He'd tried to ignore her, deny their chemistry, but she was a force of nature, someone he could not ignore. And God knows he'd tried.

Jackson left his bedroom and ran down the stairs to the hallway, trying to figure out why her *I-want-you, see-you-later* wind had changed direction. He'd left her flushed, glassy-eyed with pleasure, and he'd thought, at the minimum, that they had a fantastic night of hot sex ahead of them. What on earth could've happened between then and now to cause the frost in her voice?

This was why he stuck to one-night stands, week-long flings, Jackson thought as he strode into his barely used gourmet kitchen. If you didn't give women time to get their panties in a twist, then you didn't have to deal with the drama. And Hayley Lopez was drama personified. She was challenging and frustrating, hot and fiery and…

And he wanted her in his life for the longest time.

Jackson yanked open his fridge and stared at the mostly bare shelves, desperate to deny the thoughts that wouldn't fade. That he wanted her, that he felt more for her than he should, that all he wanted to do was to pull her into his arms, heart and life and keep her there.

Jackson slammed the fridge door shut and rested his forehead against the cool metal door. No, God, *no*. There was no way he was in love with a strong-willed, determined, opinionated woman. He'd seen what loving a willful woman did to his dad. He'd always vowed to not let the same thing happen to him.

But it had and while he had no problem following in his dad's footsteps, he'd always refused to make the same mistakes with his relationships as his dad did.

That plan hadn't worked out so well.

Jackson rubbed his hand over his jaw, reluctantly admitting that he was deep under Hayley's spell, that, if he didn't slam on brakes and skid to a halt, she had the power to emotionally destroy him. Just like his mom destroyed his dad.

Jackson was almost tempted to take that risk.

"Michaels!"

He heard his front door slam and the sound of her

boots crossing the hallway. Jackson rolled his head to relieve some tension in his neck and rolled his shoulders back. For the first time in ages, possibly the first time in his adult life, he didn't know how to deal with a woman. And the fact that she was more than a dozen years younger than him pissed him off.

He should have this under control...

It was, he decided, the Hayley Effect.

Jackson walked from his kitchen into the hallway and sighed when he saw Hayley's cold, hard face. Yep, she was in cop mode.

Awesome.

"Hayley," Jackson said, gesturing for her to enter the smallest of his three reception rooms. This house was stupidly big for one person but it was his home and it held the best memories from his childhood and teenage years spent with his dad. With its six bedrooms, theater, gourmet kitchen, study, home gym and steam and spa rooms, he rattled around in it but he couldn't bring himself to buy something smaller and leave the memories behind.

Hayley, because she was intractable, didn't move from her spot in the middle of the hall. "This isn't going to be a long conversation, so we don't need to sit." Her eyes flicked over the larger-than-life portrait of his dad that dominated the hall, her eyes lifting ever so slightly. Did she approve? Was she curious? And why did he care?

"Care to tell me why you rushed over here?"

Hayley's hand snapped up and her palm faced him

in a "just stop" gesture. "I'm not here to pick up where we left off on the side of the road!" Her nose wrinkled in distaste and Jackson sighed. *Right. Got it.*

"I never said that you were," Jackson replied. Irritated that he felt so off-balance, he jammed his hands into the pockets of his pants and stared at her. "Are you going to tell me why or am I supposed to play guessing games?"

"You bullied or bribed or harassed Bubba to sell you his land."

Wow.

"That's what you believe?" Jackson asked, feeling the first bubbles of cold anger pop in his stomach.

"That's what I know," Hayley retorted. "You left him a business card on his porch, asking him to come in and sign some papers."

"I did."

"You're not even denying it?" Hayley demanded, slapping her hands on her hips.

So far, she hadn't stated anything but the truth so Jackson just shrugged.

"I thought you heard me when I explained how important the lake was to me—is to the community! I thought that you'd shelved the development, that you'd left Bubba alone!"

"On your say-so?" Jackson raised his eyebrows. "Isn't that a little arrogant?"

"I—"

He didn't know where this conversation was going, or whether they had any type of future—he was beginning to think that they didn't—but he might as well face this issue head-on so that there would not be any future misunderstandings.

"Let's make something very clear, Hayley. You don't get to decide what I do with my business and how I do it!"

Hayley's eyes flashed with anger and disappointment. "I thought we had an understanding about the lake, Jackson. I thought you understood how important it was to me, to the community, that it stays as it is. These days, corporate entities have to be socially conscious and have respect for the environment!"

"Did you pick up that phrase on a website geared toward spoiled millennials?" Jackson sarcastically asked. "Or did you find it on a TikTok video?"

"Don't throw my age in my face!" Hayley stated through gritted teeth. "I would be this angry if I were thirty or sixty! You've no right to force Bubba out of his home! Royal does not want or need a development. And if you plow ahead with your project, the entire community will lose respect for you!"

He'd heard her, heard the feedback, and had tailored his plans accordingly. The fact that Hayley was quick to think the worst of him scorched his soul.

Hayley held out her phone. "Call Bubba, tell him that you've changed your mind."

Jackson glanced from her phone to the tight expression on her face.

"And if I don't?"

Hayley stared down at her feet, her shoulders lifting up and down in a tired shrug. He could, maybe, dismiss her words but that shrug ignited something within him. It was the same gesture his mom used to convey her frustration and distaste, and a red mist formed in front of his eyes.

"Please call Bubba, Jackson," Hayley quietly asked him, anger fading from her eyes and expression. Sad walked on in, as well as disappointed.

He could just explain but he was damned if he would. He didn't owe her any explanations, and she had no right to question him, his motivations or his decisions. And if she couldn't trust him, if she was continually going to second-guess him—just like his mother did his father—maybe they should call this over. Right now.

They were done. They had to be.

And really, they were both insane to think that a relationship between a jaded capitalist and an idealistic do-gooder could ever work.

What the hell had he been thinking?

Jackson abruptly turned and opened his massive front door and gestured for her to leave. "I think we're done."

Surprise and indecision flickered across her face. "Jackson—"

"You said what you came here to say," Jackson said, using his don't-mess-with-me-I'm-in-charge voice.

"Can we not talk about this?"

Now she wanted to talk? Jackson handed her a hard stare. "Maybe you could've led with that instead of storming into my house and laying into me," he suggested. "I've wasted enough time on this so…please go."

Hayley planted her feet and scowled at him. "What is it with you alpha males? What gives you the right to decide when a conversation is done? My father does the same thing and it's freaking annoying!"

"No, annoying is dealing with someone who doesn't have all the facts but throws temper tantrums anyway!"

Hayley's hands bunched on her hips and her scowl deepened. "That's not fair, Jackson."

Jackson gripped the bridge of his nose. "Just go, Hayley. I can't deal with this."

Hayley released a tiny hiccup, a cross between a sob, a snort and a laugh. "Of course you can't because men like you can't deal with strong women, women who have opinions, women who refuse to stand in the shadows." Hayley walked past him on her way out the door. She turned to face him and shook her head. "I'm not scared to leave, Michaels. I walked away from my father and I'll walk away from you, too. I've never been afraid to be the only one eating at my table."

Jackson watched her walk down the steps to her patrol car, parked under his portico behind his pickup truck. It looked right there, like it belonged. He shook his head and tamped down the urge to call her back, to explain, to make her his.

If he did that, he was delaying the inevitable. It might hurt a little today—or maybe a lot—but if they deepened their connection, bound her more tightly to him and he lost her, he'd fall apart. He'd seen his dad do that and he had no intention of following in his footsteps.

Jackson, unable to watch her drive away, closed his door, leaned his back against it and closed his eyes.

Alone, again.

The way it should be.

Nine

For the past week, since storming out of Jackson's house, Hayley felt like she'd been repeatedly punched in the stomach, over and over again. She recalled being eight, running into a pole and having the air knocked out of her and this felt the same, sort of, but much, much worse.

Hayley stood in front of her fridge and scowled at her shelves. Heartbreak was also the best diet. She hadn't eaten a proper meal in days. She knew that she couldn't afford to lose any more weight but neither could she make herself eat…

So she didn't. Hayley slammed her fridge door closed, figuring that she would, eventually.

Hearing her doorbell chime, she felt her heart rate kick up before cursing herself for being stupid. It wasn't

Jackson; it would never be Jackson again. Besides, she'd heard he was out of town.

For the first time since she could remember, she was lonely, and she missed him with every strand of DNA in her body. The thought of never seeing him again, not ever being held by him, kissed by him, hearing his voice, made her want to weep.

She'd shed enough tears to make Stone Lake overflow...

And she was the girl who never cried.

Hayley wrapped her arms around her torso, feeling both hot and cold and shaky. Man, how long did hearts take to heal? Would she be feeling like this next week, in a month or a year? At some point she had to start to function again—she had a job, a law degree to finish, people to help—but none of that was currently possible.

She was a wreck and despised herself for letting a mere man make her feel this way. But, Dios, what a man.

Her doorbell chimed again and Hayley sighed, resuming her walk to her hallway. She caught a glance of herself in the mirror to her right and grimaced. Lank hair, sunken cheeks, deep stripes under her eyes. She looked like something or someone Dracula had used, abused and tossed aside.

Yet she didn't care.

Pulling her door open, she stared at her parents standing on her doorstep, her mother's hand on the perfectly matched strand of pearls she habitually wore, her hair and makeup perfect. But her lips were flattened and her perfectly shaped eyebrows were pulled together in a deep frown.

Even her father looked less than debonair. His thick hair was a little ruffled and he looked harassed and worried and very unlike her normally impassive father.

"What are you guys doing here?" Hayley asked, stepping back to let them inside.

"Why aren't you answering your phone? Why aren't you checking your messages? Sheriff Battle says that you haven't been to work." Her mother touched the back of her hand to her forehead and pulled down her bottom right eyelid. "Are you sick? What's wrong? Why aren't you answering my questions?"

"She would if you gave her half a minute to do so, Inez," Hayley's dad told her before placing a kiss on Hayley's forehead. Hayley couldn't remember when last she received any affection from her dad and she stared at him, her eyes welling.

"Oh, crap, she's crying!" Juan said, placing his hand on Inez's back and pushing her forward. "You never told me there would be tears. I can't do tears!"

Hayley wiped her eyes with the ball of her hands and pushed back her shoulder blades and straightened her spine. Leading her parents into her sitting room, she told them to sit and offered them something to drink, hoping they'd refuse because she wasn't sure she had anything to give them. She'd been short of food before Jackson kicked her to the curb and she hadn't ventured near a shop, or anywhere else, since.

"I want you to sit down and tell me what's going on!" Inez told her, patting the couch next to her.

"I'm fine, Mom."

"Of course you are," Inez scoffed. "Your clothes aren't falling off you, your hair isn't a mess, your complexion is dewy and your cheeks are nice and plump. Try again, Hayley Sofia Maria Lopez."

Wow, she was using all her names. Her mama wasn't playing. Hayley didn't want to do this, not now or not ever. Her mom wasn't the sympathetic type and instead of listening and consoling her, she'd tell her she should've dated the men she tried to set her up with, that she knew best.

She'd rub salt in an already oversalted wound.

Hayley wanted to curl up into the corner of the couch, she wanted to sleep, she wanted to sob. What she didn't want to do was try to be brave in front of her demanding parents.

Maybe she could claim a wicked dose of flu. Or a strange virus...

"I can see you trying to find a way to get rid of us and it's not going to work, not this time," Juan told her, placing his still-thick forearms on his thighs, his expression intent. "I know that we've had our disagreements, sweetheart, and I drive you as nuts as you drive me, but you are still my daughter and I can see you are hurting. So, who must I kill?"

Hayley stared at him, completely shocked at his statement. "Dad! I'm a cop. You can't say things like that!"

Juan shrugged. "It'll never be traced back to me."

Hayley rubbed her temples, both pleased and scared at her father's ferocious expression and the anger in his eyes. For once, he wasn't mad at her but incandescently angry at the person who'd hurt her.

And his statement was, strangely, comforting.

Hayley watched as her mom perched on the sofa next to her dad, dark eyes boring into her. They weren't going anywhere, not until they knew why she was upset and whether she was okay.

She wasn't okay.

Hayley chose her words carefully. "I've been seeing this guy," she said, pulling her bottom lip between her teeth. "I thought we had something, but it turns out we don't."

Inez released an exasperated breath. "You're moping over a boy? I never thought I'd see the day. Maybe if you'd dated one of the boys I suggested, you wouldn't be sitting here looking like death on a plate." Inez dug in her phone for her bag, pulled it out and started squinting at the screen. "I will set you up with someone right—"

"Inez, *enough*."

Hayley stared at her father, unable to believe his harsh command. Her dad was a tough man, alpha to the max, but her mom was his soft spot and he never spoke to her with anything other than affection and reverence.

Inez looked equally shocked and if she wasn't feeling so broken, she would've smiled at her mom's fish face.

"This isn't the time, or the place, *mi alma*. Hayley needs us to listen, not to solve this for her," Juan stated, his voice firm. "As she's shown us, she's very capable of running her own life."

They both stared at him, unable to believe what they were hearing because Juan Lopez was known throughout the state, possibly the country, as being the ultimate problem-solver and trouble-shooter. He got things done…

Who was this man and what had he done with her controlling father?

"Tell us what happened, Princesa," Juan softly asked.

Right, okay. "As I said, I was seeing someone—"

"Jackson Michaels." Juan nodded.

"You knew?"

Juan shrugged, as if her question were a stupid one. And maybe it was. Her parents liked to know what their brood was doing at all times. And she was the youngest of said brood…

"I thought we had something. It turns out we don't."

"What's the problem?" Juan asked and Hayley couldn't believe that she was discussing her love life with her normally irascible father.

"What *isn't* a problem?" Hayley asked him, sounding bitter. "Firstly, he thinks I'm too young for him…"

"Pffft." Juan waved her words away. "I'm eleven years older than your mother. That's inconsequential. What else?"

"He's not interested in a relationship and if he were, he wants someone he can control and I'm uncontrollable," Hayley told him, feeling exhausted. "I'm too bold, too outspoken, too independent…"

"Too much like me," Juan added. He smiled and lifted one shoulder, his usually stern mouth lifting into a smile. "Why do you think you and I clashed so often? Of my children, you're the most like me, poor child."

Juan patted her knee before taking her cold hands in his. "Love isn't easy, *mi vida*. It's messy and hard and sometimes horrible. But it's always worth fighting for."

Hayley shook her head. "I won't beg him to love me, Dad. I…can't."

"Because if love is coerced and demanded, it's not love," Juan softly replied, understanding in his eyes. "You're right, of course you are."

"You'll be fine in a day or two," Inez told her, still looking ill at ease. Her mom was great at the practical aspects of life but struggled to express empathy or deal with emotion. "This will blow over."

Oh, and she was a terrible cheerleader.

Juan caught Hayley's eye and she thought that she caught the tiniest roll of his eyes. "*Querida*, I am very sure Hayley has no food in this house. She never eats when she's upset. Why don't you run down to the store and pick her up some food?"

"No—"

Juan silenced her protest with an I've-got-this look. He then spent the next two minutes ushering Inez out of her house, handing over keys to his beloved 1967, fully restored to original specs Ford Mustang.

When he heard the Mustang pull off, he looked at Hayley and held out his hand. "You and I? We're going for a drive."

Sick of his own miserable company, Jackson rocked up on Cammie's doorstep, hoping to share a glass of wine with his best friend after a series of shitty days. He stepped through her kitchen door—the entrance for friends and family—and lifted his eyebrows at the ultra-messy kitchen.

Cammie was the most organized person he knew and the stacks of dirty dishes, baby bottles and tins of formula scattered over every conceivable surface surprised him. He'd heard that kids could upend one's world but this was insane. Drake employed a housekeeper. Where the hell was she?

"Cam?" he called.

"Coming."

A few minutes later, Cammie, looking like she'd been pulled through a bush backward, walked into the kitchen, baby Micah resting in the crook of her arm. "Jackson? What are you doing here?" she asked, looking surprised.

"I thought I could grab a glass of wine with my best friend," Jackson suggested, noticing the stain on her long-sleeve T-shirt and that her yoga pants were splattered with a white residue.

"Six o'clock in this house is murder hour," she told him, swaying from foot to foot. "Find the wineglasses and open a bottle of red. I'll have a glass or four hundred."

"Everything okay?" Jackson asked her, his expression doubtful.

"Micah is colicky. He screams…a lot," Cammie told him. "I think I got about an hour's sleep last night, two the night before. I have never been so tired in my life."

"Where's Drake?" Jackson asked, opening a cupboard door and taking out two wineglasses.

Cammie sighed. "He's away and will be for a few more days. Mrs. Hampton's daughter had a baby, so she went to Dallas to meet her new granddaughter. But Ainsley will be home around eight. Hope I can make it that long. I never knew babies could take up so much time." She plucked at her shirt and wrinkled her nose. "I desperately need a shower but every time I put him down, he screams."

Jackson crooked his finger. "Hand him over and go take that shower."

She stared at him, astounded. "Have you ever held a baby before, Jack?"

"No, but I have held a football. How hard can it be?" Jackson told her, walking over to her. "Take a break, honey. I can look after the little guy for a little while."

She still looked undecided but transferred the small bundle into the crook of his arm, told him to support his head and bolted for the hallway before he could change his mind. A few seconds later, she came rushing back in. "If he starts to cry, there's a bottle in the warmer over there."

"I've got this."

"Or you can just pat his back…"

"You're going down the hall, not to Outer Mongolia," Jackson told her. "Go away."

Cammie narrowed her eyes at him. "And when I've showered and feel marginally human, we will discuss why you look like hell."

Jackson turned his back on her and walked Micah

over to the picture window in the kitchen, to look out onto the landscaped garden. It was cold and overcast today and the weather perfectly reflected the state of his soul.

Without Hayley in his life, he felt cold and wet, denuded. He wasn't much interested in his business, he couldn't be bothered to exercise, he felt lethargic and…blah.

Lonely and lost.

And all because a dark-eyed beauty had dropped into his life like an F-5 tornado. She'd displaced his heart, rearranged his organs, messed with his mind.

He'd been right to call it over. They didn't have a future. They were at vastly different stages of their lives: Michaels International employed excellent people and if he wanted to take a six-week trip around Europe, he could. Hayley couldn't just up and leave whenever she wanted to. And, he presumed, she used her vacation time to study.

He was wealthy and could buy, and did, whatever his heart desired. She couldn't afford designer dresses or to buy decent coffee. She had a degree to finish, her career as a lawyer to start…

And he hadn't even started to consider the difference in their personalities. Did they even matter? He was starting to think that they'd hyped their different styles to find a reason to stay away from each other, to protect their hearts.

Well, he was done doing that. Life was meant to be lived and he wouldn't be able to live his life without Hayley in it.

Jackson looked down at the bundle in his arms and looked into the pair of deep, dark wise eyes dominating Micah's little face. His skin was sallow, his tufts of hair dark and his mouth a perfect rosebud.

This was what Hayley's baby would look like...

Jackson felt his knees wobble and he tightened his hold on Micah, causing the baby to release a little squeak. Jackson ran his free hand over his face, unable to get the vision of Hayley holding a baby, his baby, off the big screen behind his eyes. He could see her, standing in his kitchen, wearing one of his shirts, legs and feet bare, hair tumbling over her shoulders and down her back, holding his child.

And it felt so damn right.

So, they'd fight. She wouldn't always agree with him, and he certainly wouldn't with her. He'd try to tell her what to do and how to do it and she'd tell him to shove it. He'd want to protect her and she'd remind him that she was the one who carried a gun...

But in between the fights and arguments, they'd laugh and talk and make sweet, sweet love and hopefully, in time, babies. She'd look at him with eyes the same shade of Micah's—big and bold—and he'd do anything, be anything for her. She'd fill his big house and his life with love and laughter and color, and his heart with joy.

He wanted to be there when she graduated from law school, support her through the grueling bar exam. He wanted to be the one who put a ring on her finger, who stood between her and her demanding parents. He'd catch their babies and, if Hayley's career took off and she wanted to work full-time, he'd cut back and work from home to be there for their kids.

He could do anything, be anything, as long as he had Hayley—his bold and beautiful butterfly—in his life.

Hayley pulled up next to what used to be her grand-parents' cottage on Stone Lake, pulled her keys out of the ignition and turned to look at her father, who sat in the passenger seat.

"What are we doing here?" Hayley asked him.

Juan gestured to the silver-blue lake stretched out in front of them. "You always liked this property, liked being here, at the lake. I thought we could take a walk along the shore."

"Why?" Hayley demanded. It was cold and miser-able on the other side of her car window and she didn't want to walk. She wanted to go home, binge a fantasy series and eat chocolates and chips. Because wasn't that what brokenhearted people did? She wasn't sure, she'd never been in love before, neither had she expe-rienced such emotional pain.

She didn't have a manual telling her how to act, what to do next.

Juan exited the car and Hayley shrugged. What the hell, they were here, her father wasn't shouting at her, so she'd take the moment.

Hayley followed him down the path to the lake and when she hit the rocky shore, she jammed her hands into the pockets of her puffy jacket, feeling the cold wind on her skin.

After walking for ten minutes in silence, Juan spoke.

"I know that you and I have had our differences, Hayley, but I am proud of what you've done and what you've achieved."

Caught off guard, Hayley darted a look at his stern face. "You are?"

"Sure. None of your brothers would've, or could've, struck out on their own and succeeded, no, flourished."

Hayley wasn't completely sure she was hearing him right. He considered her career as a cop and her studying law a success?

"Do I wish you were working for me? Of course I do. I love the idea of having all my kids under one roof, working together to expand my company.

"I'd love you to be in Dallas, to see you more often. I'd love to know that you are safe, that you live in a nice apartment, drive a nice car and wear nice clothes."

And here came the lecture…

Hayley braced herself for her father to embark on his familiar campaign to get-Hayley-back-home. Until she was back under his wing, he wouldn't be satisfied.

Hayley brushed tendrils of hair off her forehead and, instead of shutting down his suggestions, she simply shrugged. For the first time in six years, leaving Royal was a reasonable alternative. Oh, she didn't think she'd go so far as to accept a job within the Lopez group—ugh—but the nice apartment or the nice car sounded… nice. She could still be a law enforcement officer in Dallas, she could keep studying there, and Dallas had its fair share of marginalized and underprivileged people to help.

Royal wasn't the only place that needed her skills. Or her future skills.

And if she moved, she wouldn't keep running into Jackson, wouldn't be continuously slapped in the face with something she couldn't have.

"I'll think about it, Dad," Hayley told her father.

Juan laughed and put his arm around her shoulder, tugging her into his stocky body. "But you know what I want for you, Hayley?"

"For me to marry and have kids," Hayley muttered.

"No, that's your mother's dream. Believe it or not, I want you to be happy. And I don't think moving back to Dallas would make you happy. I think you need to stay here and find a way to make it work between you and Jackson," Juan told her. "I think he's a good man and someone strong enough to handle your—*our*—fiery temperament."

"Well, that's a fine idea, Dad, but he doesn't want me," Hayley told him, her voice rising. "He wants someone else, something else, but not me!"

Juan was about to reply when they saw Bubba step onto the lakeshore from the path from his house. He turned to look at them and raised his hand and waited for them to reach him.

Juan shook his hand and Hayley kissed his leathery cheek before sending him a sad smile. "I'm sorry I couldn't help you stop Jackson Michaels from developing here, Bubba. I don't know what he said or did to get you to change your mind, but nothing is legal before the papers have been signed. Have you signed his papers, Bubba?"

Bubba frowned at her. "Well, yeah."

Hayley winced. "Why didn't you talk to me first? We could've tried something else to get him off your back. It's your land. You didn't have to sell, and he can't force you to!"

Bubba looked at her like she was a mutated alien. "What are you talking about, Hayley? And why wouldn't I want to sign the papers?"

Was the world completely mad today? "Because you didn't want to sell!" Hayley yelled.

Bubba looked at Juan, lifted his hands and turned his attention back to Hayley. "That's not what happened… exactly."

Hayley rubbed her hands up and down her face, unable to keep track of this conversation. "You said you signed some papers, Bubba, papers that Jackson gave you."

Bubba nodded. "Okay, I did sell, sort of. Jackson bought my property, for a ridiculous amount of money. But I get to stay here until I die, and after that, the land will be donated to a trust Jackson set up."

A trust? "What?"

Juan rubbed his hand up and down her back. "Jackson set up a trust, Hayley. All the land he's acquired on the lake will be donated to the trust and the trust will be a public-private partnership with various partners, including the Royal municipality. He's building a running and cycling path next to the lake, upgrading the picnic and camping facilities, building decent boat ramps. The only stipulation was that the park will

be named after his dad and that no new houses can be
built on the shore."

Hayley felt like she was existing in an unfamiliar
and strange alternate reality. "I don't understand," she
told her dad.

"Jackson won't be developing the land, Stone Lake
will stay the same and Bubba will get to live out the
rest of his days in his cottage. When he dies, Jackson
will own another cottage on the lake."

"Another cottage?" Hayley demanded.

Juan smiled. "He bought your grandparents' cottage
from me a week ago."

Hayley wasn't sure how much more she could take
in. "You own, owned, whatever, the cottage? I thought
it was sold!"

"I bought it from my parents' estate," Juan told her.
"I thought that someone, at some time, would want to
develop this area so I held on to it, thinking I could
sell it for a huge profit. Which I did."

Holy smoke bombs, it was all too much.

Jackson had been planning on developing the area
around this lake. Now he wasn't. He was now going
to build a biking and cycling path for the residents to
use and name the park after his dad? Not that she had
any problem with that. His father, as she'd heard, was
a wonderful man who'd done a lot for the residents of
the town.

No, what she was having a problem with was Jackson's swinging from one position to another, him
changing his mind so rapidly. When she left his house,
he'd been harassing Bubba to sell his land...

Or was that just what she'd assumed?

"When did you speak to Jackson about him buying your property but allowing you life rights, Bubba?"

Bubba wrinkled his forehead in thought. "Ah, two weeks ago?"

Before he found her on the side of the road, before she found his business card and jumped to the wrong conclusion.

Hayley stared down at the rocks beneath her feet, wondering if she'd subconsciously sabotaged their... whatever they had. She'd been so quick to jump to conclusions, it was almost as if she wanted to find fault with him, to find a reason for him to fail. Had she been trying to protect herself because she knew that Jackson could hurt her?

It was possible. No, it was probable.

And hadn't she just shot herself in the foot? Because, despite trying to protect herself, she was still carrying around her sliced-and-diced heart.

And the reason Jackson could hurt her was that she was utterly, completely, horribly in love with the man. He was the man whose face she wanted to wake up to, whose laugh she wanted to hear, whose arms she wanted to rest within.

He was the father of future babies, her lover and her best friend.

Hayley had a million doubts about their suitability, didn't know if they could live together, knew that they would argue—a lot—but her heart wanted what it wanted and what it wanted was him.

Jackson...

But there was a good possibility that she'd blown all her chances.

"You need to talk to him, Hayley, work it out. Everything can be worked out."

Hayley lifted her eyebrows at that scorcher and Juan winced. "Everything eventually works out," he amended. "I might've taken a while to come around but here I am."

Hayley had to wonder if they'd still be having this conversation if Jackson wasn't in the picture. She folded her arms across her chest and raised her eyebrows.

"And how do you know so much about Jackson Michaels, Father dear?"

Juan simply smiled. "When your brothers mentioned the chemistry between you and him—they saw you interact at the TCC gala ball—I decided to keep an eye on the man. It's been an interesting few weeks."

"And have you been keeping an eye on me, too?"

Juan nodded and slung an arm around her shoulder. "Of course. Watching over you is what I do best."

"You've been spying on me?"

Juan rocked his hand from side to side. "*Spying* is such an ugly word."

She'd take that as a yes. Hayley rolled her eyes. "And will you ever stop?"

Juan looked at Bubba. "At what age do you stop worrying about your kids, Bubba?"

"Only when you're dead," Bubba replied before turning away and ambling off.

Hayley turned to Juan. "I'm not happy with you

and we will be having a conversation about boundaries, Father."

Juan waved her words away. "So, what comes next? Are you going to visit with Jackson and ask him for an explanation or do I need to visit with him and remind him that I own a shotgun, a shovel and sixteen backyards where I can bury his dismembered body parts?"

Hayley tipped her head to the side and hoped that her father was kidding. She was 99 percent sure he was...

She also needed to apologize to Jackson, to beg his forgiveness. For doubting him, disbelieving him, for being so damn quick to believe the worse of him.

She thought she was so damn brave, thought that her actions of walking away from her wealthy family and striking out on her own had been so courageous, but she'd always known, in the back of her mind, that she had a safety net, that she could always run home to Mom and Dad.

Going to Jackson, apologizing and telling him how she felt, would take more courage than she had, but what was the alternative?

Hating herself for the rest of her life for not taking the chance, being unable to look in the mirror because she didn't want to confront her cowardice or face her regrets? She might be young but she wasn't dumb.

What was that old saying? That, in life, we only regretted the chances we didn't leap at, the relationships we didn't make and the decisions we waited too long to take?

Ten

It would've been more romantic if she'd just rushed from the lake to Jackson's house but first Hayley needed to reunite her dad with her mom—she loved her parents but she loved them more when they stayed in Dallas and let her be—and she needed to take a shower as her hair desperately needed to be washed.

Hayley powered through her shower, hurriedly swiping a razor under her arms and down her legs, and tossing shampoo and conditioner into her hair. In her bedroom, she pulled on some fresh lingerie—she desperately needed to do some laundry—and looked for a pair of clean jeans. Pulling on a black pair, she found her left Ugg boot but the other was not visible. Dressed only in jeans, one boot and a bra, she knelt to look under her bed, desperately hoping she had a clean top to wear.

She kinda thought she didn't…

And where the hell was her other boot if it wasn't under her bed?

"Now, that's a hell of a view…"

Hayley jerked her head up at the deep voice and her forehead skimmed the ledge of the side table. She yelled, slammed her hand on her head and released a series of the more colorful curses she'd heard over the years, taught to her by veteran cops.

And criminals.

Leaning her back against the side of her bed, she looked up to see Jackson standing in the doorway to her bedroom, big arms folded, hair mussed.

"How did you get in?" Hayley asked him, pulling her fingers off her forehead to see if there was blood. There wasn't, thank goodness.

"Ah… I arrived as your dad was leaving," Jackson explained, his eyebrows pulling together. "He greeted me and then muttered something under his breath about a shotgun and a shovel?"

Nope, that didn't sound right. Mostly because her father was as subtle as a Sherman tank. "I think he was more direct than that."

Jackson winced. "Yeah, he told me that if I hurt you again, he'll blow my head off and bury me so deep that even Satan couldn't find me."

Yep, sounded like her dad.

Jackson stepped into her bedroom and held out his hand so that he could haul her to her feet. Hayley put her hand in his, and he jerked her to her feet with no effort at all. He immediately dropped her hand and Hayley felt a knife tip enter her heart. If he couldn't even hold her hand, what hope did they have?

Jackson kept his eyes on her face but waved his hand in the direction of her chest. "Get dressed and we can talk."

Hayley started to object to his peremptory command and then noticed the hot flicker of desire in his eyes, the way his eyes kept dropping to her chest. It was obvious that he was finding it difficult to concentrate and the thought charmed her...

Jackson brushed past her and picked a shirt off her bed and thrust it in her direction. "Put it on. I'll see you in the kitchen."

Jackson didn't give her a chance to respond but whipped around and left her bedroom, his footsteps heavy on her wooden floor. Tossing the shirt—she'd worn it days ago and it was less than fresh—she walked over to her closet. She flipped through her hangers and found, by some minor miracle, a white silk T-shirt. She pulled it over her head and wondered why she never wore it until she looked at herself in the mirror affixed to the inside door of the closet.

The shirt was one size too small and clung to every curve, making it look like she'd painted on the fabric. The V neck showed her cleavage, and when she lifted her arms an inch, it showed off a strip of her belly.

Hayley grimaced. Loose and dirty or tight and clean? Tight and clean won this round.

Hayley took a minute to towel dry her wet hair and

another to run a comb through the long strands, flipping her head over to scrunch her curls.

You're wasting time, Lopez, trying to delay the inevitable. Get in there, apologize, tell him you were scared because you like him more than you should, and then take his rejection on the chin.

You can do this, you have *to do this.*

Walking down her short hallway, Hayley rubbed her palms on the seat of her jeans and stepped into the kitchen to see an unfamiliar bag of coffee standing next to her cheap coffee maker. "And that?" she asked, nodding to the black-and-blue bag.

"Decent coffee," Jackson said, handing her a cup. "It's too early for liquor and I need to do something with my hands."

Touching her would be good…

Stop it, Lopez.

Jackson sent her tight shirt a sour look before lifting his cup to his lips. Hayley followed suit, sighing at the rich, dark taste. She could become addicted to the good stuff…

Just like she was addicted to Jackson.

"I was on my way to see you but why you are here?" Hayley asked him.

Jackson put his cup down on the counter and gripped the edge of the counter behind him. His gaze sharpened and his body tensed. "Why were you coming to see me?"

"Why are you answering a question with a question?" Hayley demanded, shifting from foot to foot. When Jackson didn't answer her, she released a frustrated huff. "If you must know, I was coming to apologize."

Now that she was standing in front of him, she wasn't feeling quite as brave as she did earlier, doubts washing over her in a relentless series of waves. What if he rejected her? What if he said that there was no chance? What if the sky fell in?

Hayley scratched the side of her neck. This was why it was so much easier to be single. You didn't have to second-guess yourself on a day-to-day—or, in her case, minute-to-minute—basis.

Oh, she hated apologizing. Had she mentioned that? "I wanted to say I was sorry for jumping to the wrong conclusion."

"And what conclusion was that?" Jackson asked her, sounding super polite.

Man, she'd rather walk over a bed of hot, spiky coals. "I assumed that you forced Bubba to sell you his property," Hayley admitted.

"I wish I had the skills you think I do. My job would be so much easier," Jackson said, sounding a little sarcastic.

"I saw your business card, read the message and jumped to the wrong conclusion," Hayley reluctantly admitted. "I'm sorry I didn't ask you to clarify the situation."

Jackson folded his arms across his chest and looked broody and simply stared at her like he was trying to figure something out. When he didn't speak and the silence turned uncomfortable, Hayley jumped in with another question. "My dad told me that you bought my grandparents' cottage from him?"

His eyebrows lifted and surprise jumped into his eyes. "You two are speaking?"

"Apparently so," Hayley admitted, still bemused by her dad's compassion earlier. "He and my mom came to check on me this morning because they are worried about me."

"Why are they worried about you?" Jackson demanded.

"When I'm upset, I tend to act like a turtle. I pull away and hide out."

"Why are you upset?"

"What are you going to do with my grandparents' cottage?" Hayley countered.

Jackson's harsh curse bounced off the walls. Her eyes widened as he sprung away from the counter and captured her face in his hands, his mouth covering hers in a harsh, demanding kiss. It was a take-no-prisoners kiss, a "you're mine" kiss, a kiss that belonged between the pages of an epic love story, on the silver screen.

It sent tingles to her feet and made her stomach wobble and her womb throb and her heart ache.

Hayley couldn't tell if it was the end or the beginning of something. But she did know that she didn't want it to end. Jackson's strong arms wrapped around her back, holding her so close to her body that a piece of paper wouldn't find space to slide between them. But she did know that she didn't want his kiss to end, that in his arms was where she wanted to be...

Hayley wrapped her arms around his neck, tunneled

her fingers into his hair and wrapped her tongue around his, using all her senses to imprint this moment on her psyche. The coffee taste of his mouth, the muscles in his neck under the tips of her fingers, the sound he made at the back of his throat as he took their kiss even deeper, she loved it all. She loved him…

Jackson palmed her butt and lifted her into his erection and Hayley wrenched her mouth off his and breathlessly suggested that they take this to her bedroom. They were useless communicators and were so much better at showing than telling.

Jackson squeezed her butt cheek, swiped his tongue against hers and then retreated, pulling back from her to run both hands through his unruly hair. "No."

"No?" Hayley repeated, dumbfounded. "Don't you want me?"

Jackson glared at her. "That's a stupid question. You know I do."

Hayley tipped her head to the side and eyed him, noticing the frustrated expression of his face, his flushed cheeks, his blazing blue eyes. The huge erection tenting his pants. Okay, he did want her…

"If you want me so much then why did you stop?" Hayley asked.

"Because we can't keep putting off important conversations because we get distracted by sex!" Jackson growled.

Hayley reached out to play with a button on his shirt. "Okay, then let's make it quick so that we can go to bed. You go first."

Jackson pinned her to the floor with intense eyes. "Okay, but on one condition…"

Hayley swallowed. "What?"

"After we finish a sentence, we each get to choose a piece of clothing that comes off. I bought the cottage and put it in your name. I want you to have a place of your own, somewhere you love." Jackson gestured to her chest. "Take off your shirt."

Hayley was still playing catch-up. "You bought a cottage for me? Why?" she demanded.

Jackson pulled her shirt up to her chest and over her head. "Because you love the lake and I thought that if you didn't like my house, we could live out there. Or we could use it for a weekend house. Or you could rent it out. Whatever you want to do with it, it's yours."

"I don't know what to say to that," Hayley admitted, knocked sideways. She felt a spurt of excitement at the idea of waking up in her grandparents' bedroom with its astounding view of the lake and distant hills. "Except that you can't buy me a cottage, Jackson. That's crazy."

"It's my money and I can do anything I want," Jackson told her, running his finger down her chest to hook in the front clasp of her bra. "Your turn."

"Why didn't you tell me that you were thinking of turning the land by the lake into an area the community could enjoy?" Hayley asked, tugging his shirt from the band of his pants.

Jackson shrugged. "I was going to, along with a lot of other things, the afternoon we ended things."

Jackson put his arm behind his head, grabbed his

collar and pulled his shirt over his head. Faced with all that tanned skin, Hayley immediately placed her lips on his chest, needing to taste him. When she tried to skim her mouth across his skin, Jackson's hands on her shoulders gently pushed her away.

"Your turn to confess," Jackson gruffly told her.

"I was looking for a reason to put some distance between us because you scare me," Hayley admitted. "That's why I didn't want an explanation of your message on the business card you left Bubba. I was looking for an out."

Jackson gently undid the front clasp to her bra and Hayley sighed when his big hands covered her breasts. "Why do I scare you, sweetheart?"

Hayley went to his pants and slowly pulled his belt from its buckle. "Because I feel so much for you, Jackson." She dropped the belt to the floor. "Your turn."

"You scare me, too, by the way. This thing between us terrifies me," Jackson admitted, his voice rough with emotion.

Hayley held his hips and forced her words out. "Because I am so much like your mom?"

Jackson stared at her, his eyebrows lowering into a frown. "What? No! Well, sort of."

"Well, that clears it up," Hayley wryly responded.

Jackson moved his hands from her breasts to clasp her cheeks, his thumbs gliding over her cheekbones. "You are like my mom, in some ways. You are intelligent, charismatic, forthright as hell. But, unlike her, you are not self-absorbed or demanding or manipulative."

"Good to know," Hayley murmured, relieved.

"You terrify me because you force me to be more, to not to settle for the mundane, the quiet, the easy. Because nothing about you is easy, sweetheart. A life spent with you will be a wild ride as opposed to a gentle cruise."

Did he want a life with her? Really? Hayley wanted to do a happy dance but managed to resist the temptation. Just.

Hayley dug her fingertips into the bare skin of his hip. "Do you really want a life with me?" she whispered. "I thought you didn't want to commit to anyone."

Jackson handed her a wry smile. "I've spent the last week feeling like a walking corpse. I've missed you intensely. At my lowest point, I even considered doing another U-turn on Main Street to get your attention."

"Pathetic," Hayley teased him.

"I am." Jackson dropped a kiss on the side of her mouth. "Did you miss me, Hayley-mine?"

The time for teasing was over and she needed to put up or shut up. Holding on to his wrists, she nodded. "I was coming to you tonight to firstly tell you I was sorry for being a complete bitch and secondly to ask you if there was a chance that we can make this work. I'm so in love with you, Jackson."

"I'm in love with you, too."

Hayley dropped her forehead onto his chest, overwhelmed and completely relieved. Then Jackson wrapped his arms around her naked torso and cuddled her close, his lips in her hair. Hayley breathed him in, took the moment before pulling back to look at him. The love in his eyes nearly dropped her to her knees.

"You do love me…" she said, her voice tinged with awe.

"More than I thought possible. And I always will." Jackson dropped a kiss on her nose. "You're it, for me."

"So, I'm going to be your date for any future TCC galas?" Hayley teased him.

"And for everything else," Jackson stated, opening the button on her jeans and pulling down the zipper. "Hopefully, you'll be my date for our wedding."

Hayley slapped her hand against his, her eyes wide and astonished. "You want to marry me?" she squeaked.

"That's what 'you're mine' means, sweetheart." Jackson pushed her hair off her forehead with one finger.

"Uh…huh…what?" Hayley felt the room spin and she wasn't sure why she was feeling so off-balance. She was feeling ecstatic, and scared, and wonderful, and utterly overwhelmed.

"Hayley, look at me," Jackson commanded.

Hayley's eyes met his and she saw both amusement and determination in those amazing eyes and her heart rate started to slow. "I am going to marry you, Hayley, at some point in the future. I hope we will also have children together—"

"If we don't, my mother will kill me," Hayley told him, her voice faint.

Jackson grinned. "I'm taking that into consideration." He gripped the back of her head and tilted her head up. "Marrying me doesn't mean that you have to stop being you, Hayley. I'd hate that because then you wouldn't be the woman I fell in love with. I might not be able to wait to marry you, to make you mine, but I think babies can wait for a while, don't you? You still have a law degree to finish, a career as a Legal Aid lawyer to establish. Being with me doesn't mean that you have to stop being you, sweetheart.

"From now on, we're a team and we're in this together," he added.

Hayley felt tears well and then slide down her cheek. He got her, he did. "I love you so much, Jackson."

Jackson dropped a kiss on her temple. "Excellent news. Can we get back to our game now of getting us naked?"

Hayley stepped back from him and grinned, joy invading every atom of her being. "I love you. Drop your pants."

Jackson pushed his pants down his hips and they pooled on the floor. "I love you and get those gorgeous legs out of those jeans. What plans do you have for Thanksgiving?"

"To spend it with my family. But I'm not going if you don't come with me," Hayley said, shimmying out of her jeans. "Did you really buy me my grandparents' house?"

"I did. Anything else you need? And that's a seriously sexy thong, sweetheart."

Hayley looked down at her emerald green panties, stepped out of them and swung them around her finger. His eyes deepened and she swore she heard him growl. Sexy man. "Thanks. No, I don't need anything else, just you with me. Drop those briefs, Jack."

Jackson, too slowly for her liking, pushed his hands under the band of his briefs and started pushing the fabric down. Hayley decided that if he didn't hurry up, she'd do it herself.

"I was thinking that I could buy you a truck, or you can just have mine."

She didn't care. She just wanted him naked and preferably inside her…

Wait, *what*? He wanted to buy, or give her, his limited-edition Ford 150 pickup? Her instinct was to say no, to refuse, but she knew if she did, she'd hurt his feelings. Jackson wanted to share himself with her, all that he was and all that he had, and that included his money.

If she was going to marry this man, and she sure as hell was, she'd have to put aside her independent streak and get used to his generosity. As he said, from now on they were a team.

"We have many, many, many things to discuss, including you buying me a car and me driving your Chiron, darling. But can we please do it later?"

"We can and we will. And no, you can't drive my Chiron."

Hayley pouted, knowing that her request was a long shot. "Because it's super expensive and ridiculously rare?"

"Because it's super fast and super powerful. I don't care about the car but I do care about your safety," Jackson told her. She was a protector but he was her protector, the man who would always make sure she and the kids were safe. She couldn't argue with that…

"I couldn't handle it if anything happened to you, Hayley-mine."

She was his, just as he was hers. The thought made her want to do a happy dance on the spot. "I love you so damn much."

Jackson's eyes flashed with pleasure and passion as his briefs hit the floor. And there he was, physically and emotionally naked and all hers. God, she was so incredibly lucky.

She held out her hand to him and threaded his fingers through hers. Hayley lifted his knuckles to her mouth. "I can't wait to share my life with you, to plan the rest of our amazing life together but—"

"But?" Jackson asked as she led him out of the kitchen, down the passage and into her bedroom.

She turned to face him and stood on her tiptoes to drop an openmouthed kiss on his mouth. "But right now, I need you to make love to me."

"I can do that," Jackson assured her. "Today, tomorrow, as often as I can for the rest of our lives."

It was a beautiful promise at the start of a beautiful life…

* * * * *

Look for the next book in the
Texas Cattleman's Club: Fathers and Sons
series from
USA TODAY *bestselling author Yvonne Lindsay!*

Married by Contract

Available next month!

#2845 MARRIED BY CONTRACT
Texas Cattleman's Club: Fathers and Sons
by Yvonne Lindsay

Burned before, rancher Gabriel Carrington wants a marriage on paper. But when one hot night with fashionista Rosalind Banks ends in pregnancy, he proposes...a deal. Their marriage of convenience could give them both what they want—if they can get past their sizzling chemistry...

#2846 ONE LITTLE SECRET
Dynasties: The Carey Center • by Maureen Child

Branching out from his wealthy family, black sheep Justin Carey pursued a business deal with hotelier Sadie Harris, when things turned hot fast. Meeting a year later, he's shocked by the secret she's kept. Can things remain professional when the attraction's still there?

#2847 THE PERFECT FAKE DATE
Billionaires of Boston • by Naima Simone

Learning he's the secret heir to a business mogul, Kenan Rhodes has a lot to prove. He asks best friend and lingerie designer Eve Burke to work with him, and she agrees...if he'll help her sharpen her dating skills. Soon, fake dates lead to sexy nights...

#2848 RETURN OF THE RANCHER
by Janice Maynard

After their passionate whirlwind marriage ended five years ago, India Lamont is shocked when her mysterious ex, businessman Farris Quinn, invites her to his Wyoming ranch to help his ailing mother. The attraction's still there...and so are his long-held secrets...

#2849 THE BAD BOY EXPERIMENT
The Bourbon Brothers • by Reese Ryan

When real estate developer Cole Abbott's high school crush returns to town, she has him rethinking his no-commitment stance. So when newly divorced Renee Lockwood proposes a no-strings fling, he's in. As things turn serious, will this fiery love affair turn into forever?

#2850 TALL, DARK AND OFF LIMITS
Men of Maddox Hill • by Shannon McKenna

Responsible for Maddox Hill Architecture's security, Zack Austin takes his job very seriously. Unfortunately, his best friend and the CEO's sister, Ava Maddox, has a talent for finding trouble. When Ava needs his help, he must ignore every bit of their undeniable attraction...

YOU CAN FIND MORE INFORMATION ON UPCOMING HARLEQUIN TITLES, FREE EXCERPTS AND MORE AT HARLEQUIN.COM.

HDCNM1221

The corridor ended, and he stood in front of another set of towering doors. Kenan briefly hesitated, then grasped the handle, opened the doors and slipped through to the balcony beyond. The cool April night air washed over him. The calendar proclaimed spring had arrived, but winter hadn't yet released its grasp over Boston, especially at night. But he welcomed the chilled breeze over his face, let it seep beneath the confines of his tuxedo to the hot skin below. Hoped it could cool the embers of his temper...the still-burning coals of his hurt.

"For someone who is known as the playboy of Boston society, you sure will ditch a party in a hot second." Slim arms slid around him, and he closed his eyes in pain and pleasure as the petite, softly curved body pressed to his back. "All I had to do was follow the trail of longing glances from the women in the hall to figure out where you'd gone."

He snorted. "Do you lie to your mama with that mouth? There was hardly anyone out there."

"Fine," Eve huffed. "So I didn't go with the others and watched all of that go down with your parents and brother. I waited until you left the ballroom and went after you."

"Why?" he rasped.

He felt rather than witnessed her shrug. The same with the small kiss she pressed to the middle of his shoulder blades. He locked his muscles, forcing his head not to fall back. Ordering his throat to imprison the moan scrabbling up from his chest. Commanding his dick to stand down.

"Because you needed me," she said.

So simple. So goddamn true.

He did need her. Her friendship. Her body.

Her heart.

But since he could only have one of those, he'd take it. With a woman like her—generous, sweet, beautiful of body and spirit—even part of her was preferable to none of her. And if he dared to profess his true feelings, that was exactly what he would be left with. None of her. Their friendship would be ruined, and she was too important to him to risk losing her.

Carefully, he turned and wrapped her in his embrace, shielding her from the night air. Convincing himself if this was all he could have of her—even if it meant Gavin would have all of her—then he would be okay, he murmured, "You're really going to have to remove 'rescue best friend' off your résumé. For one, it's beginning to get too time-consuming. And two, the cape clashes with your gown."

She chuckled against his chest, tipping her head back to smile up at him. He curled his fingers against her spine, but that didn't prevent the ache to trace that sensual bottom curve.

"Where would be the fun in that? You're stuck with me, Kenan. And I'm stuck with you. Friends forever."

Friends.

The sweet sting of that knife buried between his ribs.

"Always, sweetheart."

Don't miss what happens next in
The Perfect Fake Date *by Naima Simone,*
the next book in the Billionaires of Boston series!

Available January 2022 wherever
Harlequin Desire books and ebooks are sold.

Harlequin.com